MW01230487

CLEAN FREAK

Sean M. Davis

Sirens Call Publications

Clean Freak
©2020 Sean M. Davis
Licensed to and Distributed by Sirens Call Publications [2020]
www.SirensCallPublications.com

Print Edition; First Edition
All rights reserved
Edited by Erin Lydia Prime
Cover Design © Sirens Call Publications
All characters and events appearing in this work are fictitious. Any resemblance to real persons, living or dead, is purely coincidental.
ISBN: 9798676694845

This is for everyone who said I could do it. I did it.

CLEAN FREAK

Wednesday

1

Clarence tried to focus on moving the Dyson vacuum cleaner in short even strokes. He kept his elbows close to his sides so that he wouldn't accidentally touch anything in the office. The smooth back and forth motion and unvarying drone lulled him, comforted him. Still, doubt nagged him.

He hadn't cleaned the underside of the desk.

He didn't need to; he hadn't even touched it.

The name on the door was Janet Somers. Clarence loved cleaning her office. It was almost colorless, black furniture in an off-white room with a gray carpet, but there was a surprising expressionist painting in red, yellow, purple and magenta over the desk, which was infected – crawling with his germs.

Startled out of his tight concentration, Clarence realized that he had been running the Dyson over the same spot. It was going to be the cleanest 1'x3' swath of carpet on the whole floor, probably the whole building.

Clarence got his feet moving, backing out of the office so that his shoes wouldn't soil the just-vacuumed carpet. Shutting the door, he pulled out a Lysol Disinfecting Wipe from the canister clipped to his belt, the smell of artificial pine filling the hallway. It took about thirty seconds to wash the brass knob, lock and plate. It would take another thirty seconds to wipe the underside of the desk. There was still time.

Hesitating, he stared at the glistening doorknob.

He had touched only the top of the desk, he was sure of it, and he'd thoroughly wiped it down afterwards. If he went back into the office, he'd need to sanitize everything he touched and vacuum the floor again. Plus, Mr. Caruthers had already yelled at him twice this week.

The desk was mass-produced office furniture, particle board with a plastic veneer that made it look like dark-stained wood, but the underside was unprotected. There was nothing to stop his germs from finding a million crevices in which to grow, multiply, spread, infect.

"Clarence!" Mr. Caruthers, the Haimes Building evening manager, stomped down the hallway, the stairwell door swinging shut behind him.

Mr. Caruthers had been doing paperwork at his desk in the basement when motion had caught his eye on the monitor showing the north hallway on six. Clarence had come out of the second office from the end of the hall as Mr. Caruthers had checked his watch. Swearing, he'd left the paperwork half-done and climbed the stairs up to the sixth floor. His claustrophobia would never survive a ride in the elevator, and besides, it was good exercise.

Seeing Clarence made his jaw clench and his left arm ache. The compliments Mr. Caruthers received from Arrow Solutions on five and Argent, Lake, and Dewey on six about the janitor were hardly worth this aggravation.

Clarence brushed his wispy, blond hair out of his face, and pushed his gold-rimmed glasses up on his nose. They immediately slipped back down to where they always sat. Mr. Caruthers stopped, his protruding stomach almost touching Clarence, who pressed his palms flat against his thighs. The cotton of his slacks was worn there, smooth under his hands.

"It's seven o'clock." Mr. Caruthers paused, even though it wasn't a question. "It's seven o'clock, and you've cleaned two offices."

"Yes, Mr. Caruthers," Clarence said.

While Mr. Caruthers was here, he may as well kill another bird. "And you stayed late again last night."

"Yes."

Mr. Caruthers wiped the sweat from his forehead. "You can't keep staying late."

"I punched out," Clarence said. He turned red and he looked down at his shoes.

"I know that!" Mr. Caruthers snapped. The way Clarence stood so rigid with his shoulders drawn up to his ears unnerved him, which made him mad. "That's the point! You can't work off the clock. Liability. *And* the Labor Department would be all over us!"

Clarence stood silent, not rolling his eyes or looking away like Mike or Val might, but attentive to the reaming he received. He listened and seemed to understand, but nothing ever changed.

Clarence's lack of response irritated Mr. Caruthers. Even a stammered, feeble excuse was better than nothing. Mr. Caruthers was about to lay into him, but then Clarence's stomach gurgled. In the after-hours office, it sounded like a dog growling.

Blushing, Clarence mumbled, "Sorry."

His eyebrows pulling together and drawing down, Mr. Caruthers asked, "When were you planning on taking a dinner break?" The question made him feel like this guy's fucking father.

"Well, sir," Clarence said, his voice barely audible. "I thought that since I was behind, I'd—"

"You have to take a dinner break." A headache was building pressure behind Mr. Caruthers's eyes, making them throb. "You are working more than six hours, and we are required by law to give you one paid fifteen-minute break and one unpaid half-hour break."

Clarence bowed his head. Even if he hurried, it would take him another two hours minimum to clean all of the executive offices on the sixth. They had so much furniture to dust behind and vacuum underneath, and potted plants in practically every corner. Studies had shown that the flu virus can live up to forty hours on the leaves of a fern.

"Mr. Caruthers, may I finish cleaning this floor, and then I'll take my dinner break?"

"I don't give a damn when you take it. I just want you to do two things for me." He held up his index finger. "Take your dinner break." Adding his middle finger, he said, "And finish your work by midnight!"

"Yes, sir," Clarence said to Mr. Caruthers's broad back as he turned on his heel.

Clarence watched Mr. Caruthers walk down the hall. His father had been like that too: yell and walk away. Clarence didn't want to disappoint him anymore. He'd clean the fifth and sixth floors of the Haimes Building by midnight, and it didn't matter that he hadn't cleaned the underside of Janet Somers's desk because he hadn't touched it.

Clarence frowned as he gathered up the power cord of the vacuum, pulling it while pushing his janitor's cart. At the next office, he unclipped his keys from his belt. Popping the top on the Lysol Wipes canister, he cleaned his master key, unlocked the door, pushed it open, wiped the knob, and turned on the light.

Starting at the desk, he pulled the chair out, wiped it down, and shoved the towelette into the bag hanging on his belt. With his other hand, he unhooked the Swiffer Duster. His knees together and shoulders scrunched, Clarence stood on the balls of his feet. Leaning over the desk, he supported himself with his hand on the desk top, which was okay, because he was going to clean it anyway. He dusted the back of the computer monitor, behind it and three framed pictures of smiling people, then their fronts. Straightening up, Clarence froze.

The heel of his hand rested on the top of the desk, his fingers curled over the edge. He'd cleaned Janet Somers's desk this exact same way, but he was sure he hadn't—

He had, and even worse. Clarence had been dusting the monitor and gotten a tickle in his throat.

He'd coughed lightly into his hand, as his mother had taught him. Then he'd bent over the desk to finish the job, his hand on the desk, fingers curled over the edge, touching the exposed particle board.

It would be fine. Besides, Mr. Caruthers was counting on him. He had the rest of this floor and another to clean by midnight and he couldn't waste any more time.

Tomorrow, Janet Somers would walk into her office, sit at her desk and grip the edge, pulling her chair in. She'd rub her tired eyes and yawn widely, a polite hand over her mouth. She might eat a granola bar for a mid-morning snack, or even eat lunch at her desk, without washing his germs off of her hands and get sick, just like—

Sweat dotted Clarence's forehead. His breath clogged in his throat. His eyes prickled. He pushed his glasses up onto his forehead and wiped his eyes, stumbling to the door. Out in the hall, he sprinted the few steps to Janet Somers's office. Seizing the doorknob, he rattled it in panic turning to fury before he realized it was locked. Grabbing his key ring from his belt, he stabbed at the lock, rammed the key in, twisted it and threw the door open.

His heart hammered and white threads pulsed across his tear-blurred vision. Lurching toward the desk, a square of light following him through the door, Clarence fumbled with the stiff bristle brush and spray bottle of Lysol Multi-Surface clipped to his belt.

Shoving the rolling chair aside, Clarence fell to his knees. He stuck his head under the desk, craned his neck around so he could see, sprayed and then started scrubbing. The smell tickled his nostrils. His throat opened and he sighed deeply. His heart rate slowed, returning to normal, as he scrubbed harder, faster. The sweat dried on his forehead, chilling him, and he blinked his eyes clear. Finally satisfied that his germs were expunged, Clarence crawled backward and rose, first to his knees, then to his feet.

Removing his glasses, he mopped his face on the sleeve of his uniform polo, replacing them and pushing them up his nose. They slid down and he tilted his head up so he could see.

He'd touched the chair, the door, walked on the carpet, and couldn't take the chance that he hadn't touched the top of the desk. Its analog hands glowing green, the clock on the wall read seven eighteen, no second-hand, but time racing anyway. His head drooped and Clarence trudged out into the hallway to retrieve his Dyson. Mr. Caruthers would be disappointed, mad. But Janet Somers would be okay, and that's what was important.

After cleaning up after his mistake, Clarence moved as fast as he could. His stomach kept rumbling while he finished cleaning the offices. Then, he washed the walls of the hallway, dusted the air vents and vacuumed his way to the elevator. After he took his janitor cart and Dyson down to the fifth floor, he continued down to the basement, hungry and frustrated with himself.

It was quarter after nine, which meant that after his break, he'd only have two hours and fifteen minutes to clean the whole fifth floor. In a perfect world, he'd be allowed to work without interruption, free from the constraints of a time clock or his stomach. Smiling, Clarence imagined lingering over every flat surface, enjoying the pure smell of a truly clean place.

Like his apartment. He'd spent the morning humming along with the vacuum cleaner, beat boxing with the hiss of the spray bottles. He'd had lunch while scanning the noon news programs, but none of the stories interested him. He'd spent an hour on the computer searching for the best way to clean Tiffany glass, just in case he ever got a piece. Then he'd taken a second shower, cleaned the bathroom, and spent the rest of the afternoon reading.

The elevator slowed, chiming its arrival. Clarence hated the Haimes's basement. Its concrete walls weren't properly sealed and it always stank of mold, despite the grinding hum of an overworked de-humidifier. The door slid open. Mike and Val were standing there laughing, but they stopped when they saw Clarence.

The three janitors were assigned to different floors, but Mike and Val had decided that it was quicker and more fun to work together. Mr. Caruthers didn't care because they got their work done with few problems. One day last year, a month after Val had started working in the building and the same week she and Mike had teamed up, she'd asked him about Clarence.

"Think he'd wanna get in on this?" she'd

asked, gesturing at the two of them and around at the third floor's reception area they were cleaning.

"You can ask him," Mike had replied, "but I know what he's gonna say."

"Bet you don't."

"Bet you a shot." Mike, who had been working with Clarence for two years, had felt almost guilty for scamming Val.

As Mike had predicted, when Val had pitched the idea to Clarence, she'd received a quiet and polite "No, thank you."

Clarence had been appalled. Working in such close proximity with them terrified him, not only because he might infect them. He walked through the first-floor lobby every night. Clearly, his and their definitions of clean were worlds apart.

Val was the first to break the shocked moment of silence in the basement. She looked down and saw Mike's hands hanging at his sides. She lunged. Before he could react, she slapped his hand. Mike groaned, shoving them into his pockets. Clarence gasped, jerked backward as if she'd slapped him.

Val laughed at Mike. "Ha! That's three to one! Look like you buying tonight!"

"Night's not over," Mike said. "Hey, Clarence, uh—"

The elevator chimed and the chrome door started sliding shut. Mike dove forward and grabbed it. Clarence yelped and jumped back, colliding with the rear wall. The door stopped, reopened, and Mike and Val crowded in. Clarence dodged away from them, struggling with his Lysol Wipes canister as they stepped to the rear of the elevator.

"Clarence, man," Mike said, "you getting out?"

"No. Yes. No. I—uh…"

"If you're getting out, get," Val said, pressing the button for the third floor. To Mike, she said, "Wait. We done on three?"

"Eh, done enough."

The wipes hadn't torn along their perforations. Clarence held one end of a rope of them, trying to get at the rear wall, unable to get around them.

Then, the door was closing again, forcing Clarence to make a decision. Thirty seconds in an unclean elevator was risky, but they probably wouldn't touch the walls, and he'd already wiped the floor buttons clean. Riding with him was more serious. Twisting his body to avoid touching Mike and Val, the walls, or the door as it closed, he jumped out.

Their confused expressions changed as they turned to each other, already talking, their words muffled, then vanishing as the elevator rose. Clarence took a step back, watched the floor lights above the elevator. When the **B** went dark and the **1** lit up, he pushed the call button. He waited, twisting the Lysol Wipes in his hands, tiny rivulets of cleaning solution dripping down his wrists.

Clarence could have worn gloves—had worn gloves, the epiphany coming to him when he'd been fourteen. He had immediately raided his piggy bank for five dollars and nineteen cents, enough for a pair of Rubbermaid gloves, yellow, his favorite color. Eight days later, he'd soaked them in bleach and thrown them away, his hands covered in blotchy red sores which cracked and bled. The cold water he'd run his hands under had temporarily soothed but eventually chapped them even worse. Clarence couldn't quarantine his germs; they would rot him. His only choice was to clean up after himself, as his mother had advised, and hope that no one else would die because of him.

As the elevator's door opened on the empty third floor, Val asked, "What's his deal, anyway?"

Mike shrugged. "I don't freaking know." He exited the elevator, his steel-toed boots whumping on the rug.

Val's sneakers whispered as she followed. "He's weird."

"Think?"

Val paused and scratched her nose, her left hand hanging at her side. "His belt's cool. Where'd he get it?"

"Don't freaking know." Mike slapped at the hanging hand.

She'd seen him looking and he wasn't even close. "Haw haw!" she Nelson-laughed. "Too slow! You're never gonna catch up by midnight." Val put her hands in the kangaroo pocket of her hoodie, thinking while Mike growled in frustration. "Why does he do that with his hands?"

"What?"

Val demonstrated, hunching her shoulders and putting her hands on her thighs.

"I don't freaking know," Mike said, keeping his eyes on them.

Val saw and put them back in her pocket, continuing down the hallway. "Bet it'd be hard to steal a five."

Catching up to her, Mike said, "Yeah, probably."

Their vacuum and janitor cart were in the last office. It was about nine-twenty. They could probably be done by eleven, then have an hour to kill before clocking out and heading to the bar.

Beside him, Val stopped again, so he did too. Under the half-dimmed fluorescents, an I-have-an-idea expression lit her eyes and she was grinning, kind of laughing. Mike groaned. The last time she'd had that look, they'd been written up for racing on their carts.

Mike opened his mouth to say, "No. Whatever it is, no."

Before he could get a word out, she slapped his hand.

"Four-one. Clearly, you suck at this. Or maybe I just rock that much. Probably both. Point is, I'm getting bored and you're going broke."

Mike smiled, turning away to hide it. She did care about him. Sometimes her sarcasm and teasing made it hard to tell.

"But Clarence," she continued, "is a challenge to both of us. So here it is: we call truce and go after Clarence and the first to steal a five is the ultimate champion of the universe!"

His smile widened to a nicotine-yellow grin.

Thirty-four-years-old and she was still fun and cool, not like the chicks Mike went to college with, who took themselves too seriously and couldn't even take a freaking joke.

He gave her a high five and said, "You're on!"

2

Clarence had been so close, even after needing to clean the elevator. He'd only had four offices and the sixth floor hallway left to clean when Mr. Caruthers had stopped him at midnight, told him to go home. Clarence had pleaded with him, but Mr. Caruthers had ignored him, saying that he was lucky that he wasn't being written up. His boss had marched him out of the building and locked it behind him.

But Clarence had keys and knew Mr. Caruthers' alarm code, and it'd been just a matter of driving around for ten minutes until he no longer saw his boss' car in the parking lot. Inside, the red lights of the cameras had been difficult to ignore, but he hugged the walls where he could, hiding from their blinking red lights and glass eyes.

He'd gone back up to the sixth and worked by the orange glow of the arc-sodium lights shining in from along the freeway service drive. Now that he didn't have Mr. Caruthers looking over his shoulder, he was able to clean things the way they deserved to be. After he finished, he stood waiting for the elevator and breathed deeply, the wonderful clean smell hanging fresh in the air. Then, the elevator opened behind him and took him down to the dank basement, then out the door.

The drive from the Haimes Building in Southfield to Detroit's northwest side was short, especially at three in the morning. Most of the hardcore drinkers that closed bars even on Wednesday nights were already sleeping it off at home. Even so, Clarence drove with his hands at ten and two, leaning forward in his seat, his left foot poised above the brake pedal.

Clarence eased his foot off the gas, merging onto another freeway. A Cutlass Supreme swerved around him, making him clutch the steering wheel, a subwoofer momentarily thudding bass in his solar plexus. The rest of the drive home was uneventful, and Clarence turned into the Applewood Apartments' parking lot near the corner of Grand River and Outer Drive a short time later.

He parked his Pontiac in his car port. After wiping the steering wheel, he opened the door and knelt next to the car. Using the cordless Dirt Devil he kept in the back seat, he vacuumed off the seat and floor. Another Lysol Wipe to clean the pedals, interior of the door, and vacuum.

Walking to his building, a brisk November wind blew dried leaves around his feet. Clarence imagined leaving a pale green trail, which smeared together with the trails of other people, making it a miracle that people weren't dying from the germs they waded through every day. His key was out and wiped clean, the door unlocked and opened, the doorknob sanitized and the door closed behind him before the enormous implications left his mind.

The hum of his air purifiers greeted him. He inhaled deeply, then exhaled in pleasure. In the dark, Clarence's shoulders relaxed. A small smile bloomed as he clapped twice. The two lamps on either end of the sofa burst into light, glowing on the golden yellow walls. His smile blossomed as he remembered walking through this door for the first time, five months ago.

He'd gasped. Bob O'Neil, Applewood's property manager, had been quick to say, "Of course, if you don't like the color, we can certainly have—"

"No, no!" Clarence had said, turning a circle in the living room. "It's perfect. And it's so," a brief, rapturous pause, "clean."

"Well, we had to be thorough," Bob O'Neil had said, then flinched, his teeth clicking. Clarence hadn't noticed, still almost dancing in delight.

Clarence undid his janitor's belt and hung it on a hook by the door. He walked around the half-wall of the entryway, glanced at the kitchen out of habit, not hunger. Instead, he continued down the hallway to the bathroom. Across from the bathroom was a second bedroom, his office and reading room, the walls were the soothing pale purple of lilac.

In the bathroom, he undressed, folding his clothes before placing them in the hamper. The bathmat was pastel yellow and fuzzy under his feet, the lime mint smell of his previous showers lingering in the matching curtain and towels. He turned on the hot water as far as it would go. Steam flushed his pale skin.

Clarence stepped in on the end opposite the showerhead. The water thrummed on the tub, spattering burning flecks onto his feet and ankles. Clarence stood, sweat dribbling down his face and body. His limp hair clumped with moisture. He was filthy, contagious and disgusting. His head hung in shame.

His shampoo was deep cleaning, his body wash triple action. They smelled like limes and mint, crisp and clean. He washed himself from the head down. Squinting through the suds, he ducked under the cascading water.

He grunted, clenching his jaw. The water sloughed the lather from his body and hair. The water turned a pale green, running down the drain. He rinsed himself as quickly as possible. Then, he shut the water off and stood for a moment, panting. His angry red skin radiated heat, but he smiled. He was clean, if only for a few minutes.

Pulling aside the curtain, he grabbed a fresh towel from the stand next to the shower. He dried himself, then folded it and placed it in the hamper atop his clothes. Then, he dressed in clean pajamas.

From beneath the sink, he got Comet Cleanser, Lysol Tub and Tile, and a brush. He cleaned the shower from the top down, then sprinkled the powdered bleach in the tub and knelt next to it. He started scrubbing. Beneath the comforting sound of stiff bristles scratching came a soft gurgling from the drain.

Clarence paused, thinking that maybe he was just overtired and hearing things, but the sound, a girl crying softly, continued.

He scooted over, leaning close to the drain. "Hello?" The crying cut off. "Hello? Is someone there?" Clarence whispered louder. Silence, then the crying resumed. Still louder, he asked, "Are you in the next apartment? What's your name?"

The crying stopped again, then the single word, "Lucy," reverberated from the drain.

Clarence hesitated, then asked, "Are you okay?" When she didn't answer, he asked, "Why are you crying?"

She still didn't say anything, and the silence lasted so long that he started to sit back.

Then, she said, "Once upon a time in a faraway kingdom, there lived a king with his queen, and they had a daughter, Princess Lucy, who was the most beautiful little girl in the whole world."

Clarence leaned forward, smiling indulgently as he pictured the little girl telling the story.

"The girl had black hair, and brown eyes like chocolate, and when she laughed, birds sang. Friends of the king and queen came from miles and miles around to see the little princess. This made the queen jealous.

"The queen was beautiful like the princess once upon a time, and the people that visited them told the princess that she looked like her mother, but the princess didn't think so.

"The queen was ugly and old and wrinkled and didn't look like the pictures the king showed the princess. People stopped coming over because the queen would cry after they left and spend a long time looking in the mirror.

"It was the queen's jealousy that made her

ugly, and being ugly made her mean. She made the princess clean the castle all day, wouldn't let her play outside in the apple orchard, and wouldn't even let her go to school."

Clarence was about to speak up to tell Lucy that cleaning wasn't a punishment, but then the little girl shrieked in a high-pitched cracking voice that made Clarence jump back.

"'What can she learn in school that I can't teach her?' the queen would scream at the king. The king was a kind man who didn't like to argue, so he let the queen have her way."

Clarence shifted his weight, picturing Lucy's mother, black hair like the princess, white streaks like Frankenstein's bride. He empathized with the king. When his mom had yelled, it had always made him feel guilty.

"The queen knew that if the princess went to school, she'd be able to outsmart her someday, so she kept her home and made her clean the whole castle everyday by herself, and when she tried to sing for the birds to come and help her, the queen yelled at her to stop her fairy tale nonsense."

Clarence cocked his arm up on the edge of the tub and lowered his face near the drain. Lucy's voice had gotten quieter and he could barely hear her.

"She was very lonely." She said, "She just wanted someone to be her friend!"

Clarence jerked back, bumping his head against the door that led through his walk-in closet to his bedroom.

"When the king returned from court every day," she continued, "he didn't know what was going on, so he thought everybody was happy. The princess tried to tell him about the queen's evil one day, but he just grunted and told her she should listen to her mother.

"That's when she realized that the queen was actually a witch and was controlling the king with her magic. The princess needed to do something.

"She watched the queen carefully. The queen spent a lot of time in the bathroom, and it didn't take long for the princess to figure out that the bathroom mirror was magic. The queen would stare at it for hours, muttering spells, and bang her hands on it when they wouldn't work.

"The magic mirror needed to be destroyed. It was the queen's strength and her only weakness."

Clarence nodded, picturing the evil queen in Snow White.

"There was a metal frog on the coffee table," Lucy said. "It was really heavy and hard to move to clean under it, and one day, the princess got an idea.

"The queen was trying to get one hard spell to work and it wasn't. She kept saying, "It's not supposed to be this way," over and over, and banging her hands on the glass and the princess hoped that it would break without needing to do anything. But the queen got tired of hitting the mirror and yelling, so she went into her room and shut the door.

"The princess stood outside until she heard the queen snoring, then she ran and got the frog and came back to the bathroom and—"

Clarence wanted to urge her to go on, but couldn't say anything when he heard her crying again.

"The mirror was trying to scare the princess," Lucy said. "It showed her in it, but she was ugly and scary and had red eyes and claws and she almost ran away, but then she threw the frog, and it broke the mirror!"

Clarence flinched. The broken glass would have gone everywhere, such a dangerous mess. The fog on his bathroom mirror had evaporated.

"The princess ran into the queen's room shouting, "Mommy, mommy, we're free!" The queen hugged the princess tight, squeezing her until she almost couldn't breathe."

Clarence was having trouble breathing. He'd left the shower only half-cleaned.

"The queen told the princess that special girls deserve a special bath, so go get Ducky. The princess didn't want to take a bath, but she knew it didn't do any good to argue with the queen. She went to her room and grabbed Ducky and kissed him, but he didn't turn into a prince, so she had to take a bath."

The Comet and Lysol Tub and Tile he'd used had dried to a thin, brittle crust while Clarence sat listening to Lucy. His germs hadn't been washed down the drain. A few had undoubtedly survived and were now multiplying, spreading.

Clarence's legs had fallen asleep and he stumbled to his feet. "Hang on a second Lucy. I need to finish cleaning the shower."

"Wait!" Lucy tried to say, but Clarence had turned on the faucet, drowning her voice.

Steam rose and Clarence held his filthy hands under the water, drawing a sharp breath. The crusted bleach dissolved. When he couldn't stand the temperature any longer and they felt clean again, he removed the shower head and rinsed off all of the Lysol and Comet, which rushed down the drain in a gurgling, green tide.

Calmed down, Clarence shut the shower off. Kneeling next to the tub again, he leaned over, his hands behind his back, careful not to contaminate what he'd just cleaned.

"Hello?" he called. Water dripped onto the side of his face, ran down and off his chin. The drain was silent, not even the sound of water running down.

She must have gone to bed, Clarence reasoned, yawning. It was late, after all.

Pumping some moisturizing sanitizer into his hands, rubbing them together, Clarence crossed the hall to his bedroom. A quick clap turned the lamp on. He pulled back the covers, sat on the edge of the bed and swung his legs in. Settling into his usual position, he clapped again and the light went out.

Before his eyes could adjust, the dark room closed in around him, tight and almost suffocating. He stared into the empty space that was just beyond the bed but that stretched into forever. Then, memory combined with the muted light from the street lamps through the blinds to color his room a deep shade of red. The sheets that had been cool against his skin started to warm. He blinked slower and slower, his chest rising and falling shallower each time. One last, deep breath that flowed out of him as his eyes slipped closed and he was at the door that the world fell through on its way to somewhere else.

His mother laid in the hospital bed, a respirator taped into her open mouth. When she breathed, she sounded like a congested drain, the water only able to glug and gargle. Clarence stood next to her bed, not holding her hand. She groped for him, an IV in her arm and a hospital bracelet around her wrist, but Clarence stepped back, away from his mother.

"I'm sorry, Mom," he said, tears stinging his eyes, his father nothing but hands on his shoulders, neither cruel nor caring.

In real life, his mom had said nothing, the respirator blocking all communication and the pain killers numbing all comprehension. Now, she said, "You should wash your hands more often," and the steady beep that had been so easy to ignore turned into a monotonous tone. Men and women in white and pale green rushed in and his father pulled him along in a nothing-more-to-see-here kind of way. Clarence turned around swinging, hands held splayed, wanting to kill his father too.

His father caught his arms, slapped him twice across the face, forehand, backhand, and Clarence was pulled along, out of the hospital into a gray world that turned black.

Behind them, in a room that had smelled of impotent cleanliness, the damage having already been done, orderlies removed the machines of life from Clarence's mother and pulled the sheet up over her face.

Thursday

3

There was something wrong.

It wasn't the light, gray and muted, filtered through Venetian blinds and closed eyelids. It was November gray, Michigan gray, and not the other gray that fringes the edges of memories and dreams. It wasn't that Clarence was uncomfortable. He was chilled, but in the way that he could tell through the window that it was cold outside. It wasn't the feeling that he wasn't alone.

Clarence snapped awake, covered in a light sweat turning cold as he thrashed out from under the covers. Six running steps took him into the bathroom.

He twisted the hot water knob until it wouldn't turn any further. Starting the shower, he pulled his shirt over his head, not bothering with the buttons, pushed his pajama bottoms down and kicked them off. He lurched into the shower. Tears that felt cool on his skin mingled with the scalding water. He stood under the water as long as he could bear, letting the sweat rinse from his body, then washed, rinsed and turned off the shower. Clarence shivered in the comparatively freezing air. He snuffled.

It always starts with a stuffy nose, his mom would say. Blow your nose regularly and you won't get sick.

Clarence stepped out of the shower, still dripping. There were no tissues in the bathroom, so he tore off some toilet paper, steadied himself after a violent tremor, and blew his nose. Mucus shot out and soaked the Charmin, splitting it. He yelped, elbowed the toilet seat up and dropped the dripping toilet paper in. Then, he washed his hands. Again and again, until he couldn't feel his diseased slime on his palm.

His pajamas were in a crumpled pile on the floor. The shower needed to be cleaned. His diseased tissue floated in the toilet and he couldn't forget that his bed was filthy with his fever sweat. Clarence's body thrummed and his hands twitched.

Might as well start with what was right in front of him, so he picked up his pajamas, folded them and put them in the hamper. Already, he felt a little better. Next, he flushed the toilet, opened the cabinet under the sink and retrieved the bottle of Lysol Toilet Deep Clean.

After the toilet was clean, Clarence cleaned the shower. On his hands and knees scrubbing, he felt almost dizzy with déjà vu. He stopped and leaned closer to the drain. Remembering, he pulled his head back as the faucet dripped, the water plunking on the porcelain. There were no other sounds.

Clarence finished and rinsed the walls and tub, mesmerized by the sound of running water, but then he thought about his sweat-soaked sheets. That broke his trance.

Clarence dressed in khakis and a button-up, short-sleeved shirt. He put his glasses on and pushed them high on his nose. They promptly slid down to their accustomed place.

Whenever he was sick as a child, which was often, on the first day he was able to go back to school, he'd come home to a fresh, almost-like-new bed. His mother would have washed the sheets, blankets, pillows and mattress pad, which was fine, but not enough. He'd always get sick again and now, years later, he knew why. Not that he blamed his mother. He blamed himself.

Clarence stripped the bed down to the mattress. Carrying the whole heap, he walked to the laundry room, which was housed in a separate building four doors down. Luckily, all three machines were free, one for sheets and pillows, one for blankets and the last for the mattress pad. After starting them, he pulled out a pocket-sized package of wipes and cleaned the coin slots and lids of the machine, as well as the door handle on his way out.

Back in his apartment, he unfurled the steam-cleaner and cleaned his mattress. That was the part that his mother hadn't known to do, the reason he'd gotten sick again and again and again. But he knew better now thanks to a blog article, "4 Reasons Why Clean Sheets Aren't Enough."

Clarence still needed to wash his dirty clothes and clean the apartment, but he felt so much better than when he'd woken up. Today might turn into a good day, after all.

While his sheets were being washed, he cleaned the apartment. The air purifiers droned and

Clarence hummed along with them contentedly.

Putting the vacuum cleaner into the closet, after a wipe down, he grabbed the Clorox bleach and dryer sheets and went to the laundry room. Shivering against the chill air, he sanitized his hands, rubbing them together to try and warm them, before touching the door to go inside. His humming turned into Sweet Emotion by Aerosmith as he moved his bedding from the washing machines to the dryers.

After making the transfer, he put more quarters into the washing machines, starting them on the heavy cycle. Still humming, he poured bleach into each machine.

As he was pouring Clorox into the last machine, the door creaked open behind him. It was a woman that he'd seen around, but hadn't ever talked to. She looked completely different from her usual khaki and green shirt that must be her work uniform in her Capri pants that were too scanty for the weather and jacket pulled tight around her, a laundry basket under one arm. Her face fell as she saw Clarence standing at the machine, heard the others churning.

"Ah, shit," she said. Looking out from beneath lowered eye lashes, she said, "I'm so sorry to have to ask this, but I thought I had one more clean shirt, but I don't and I would just wear the one from yesterday, but everything smells kinda ripe and I need to be to work in an hour. Can I maybe just use one of the machines now? I can reimburse you."

She had blonde hair and dark lashes that brought out her pale blue eyes. Her smile looked like her best weapon, one she used often. Clarence opened his mouth, but nothing came out.

The woman's eyes flicked down to the open machine which was still filling. "Hey—aren't you doing laundry?"

"I—"

"What are you doing? You already put bleach in there?" she demanded. "Fuck! I'm gonna be late! What the fuck are you doing?"

She stepped forward, challenging. Dropping the Clorox bottle, which landed on its side, Clarence shrank away, re-sanitizing his hands. The sharp smells of bleach on top of alcohol made the woman crinkle her nose. She spun on her heel, still muttering to herself as she walked toward the door.

"God damn it and now I have to go to the Coin-Op and I won't have time to wash my hair and what's the good of wearing a clean shirt when my hair smells like barf? Jesus, I knew I shouldn't have gone out last night. Who goes out on a fucking Wednesday—?"

"I'm sorry," Clarence murmured, not expecting the woman to hear. But she did.

Turning, she demanded, "What?"

Pushing his glasses up on his nose, he said, only a little louder, "The machines were dirty."

She stood, like she didn't understand. Clarence tried to smile, the corners of his mouth barely lifting. The woman sneered, or grimaced at the pervading smell of bleach, which still glugged out onto the floor. Clarence couldn't tell.

"Fucking freak." She slammed the door behind

her.

Clarence felt sad, not angry. Everyone was a slave to their schedules, rushing around without the time to attend to the basic needs of cleanliness. He picked up the Clorox jug, which was only trickling now that half of it had spilled out onto the floor. The washing machine filled with an agonizing slowness, the hot water steaming off of the metal drum.

He did wish that he could stop her from going to the Laundromat. Baskets and baskets of dirty clothes, women and children buzzing around like flies, unshaven men with dark sweat-stains under their arms. She would almost certainly get sick, go to work, spread it amongst her co-workers, who would then go home to their families and cause an epidemic and it would all be Clarence's fault.

4

It was one thing for Mike and Val to have talked about it at the bar last night. It was another to be standing in Mr. Caruthers's doorway as he stared, his mouth pulled down into a toad's grimace waiting for a reason, an explanation, even a friendly hello. Val elbowed Mike in the side and he whuffed, trying to think of how they'd come up with the plan last night. At the time, it had seemed ingenious, but now he couldn't remember what in the hell had made him think that.

"Go ahead," Val whispered.

"It was your idea," he may as well have said out loud. Whispering didn't do much good in the small, silent office.

Val elbowed him again.

Mr. Caruthers cleared his throat. The office was small, almost too small for his large frame. The desk, chair and two filing cabinets crowded the floor space and the only window was an impenetrable glass block near the ceiling that didn't even give a decent view of the sidewalk. Add to that, these two knuckleheads filling the doorway, cutting off his only escape route if the walls started closing in.

"Look, you two. I don't know what you're up to, but I don't have time for it. Clarence is late and—"

"Yes!" Mike said. His boss twitched back in his

chair, surprised. "Well, me and Val, we got to talking last night. Seems that Clarence gets the short end, the two of us working together. You know how we can just get into that groove and really get shit done? Stuff! Get stuff done."

Mr. Caruthers's expression was unchanged. Mike opened his mouth to continue, but was interrupted. "The point, please, Mike. I don't need a play-by-play."

"Well, anyway, me and Val got to talking, and we thought that if two are enough to get four floors done without any trouble, then the three of us should be able to do the whole building, no problem."

"Three?"

"Yeah." Then, realizing he'd left out a big chunk of the thought process, he said, "Me, Val and Clarence."

Clearing his throat again to cover that he was finding it difficult to breathe in the shrinking office, Mr. Caruthers stood and took a step toward Mike, trying to seem casual. Caught by surprise, Mike stumbled back, but before he could, Mr. Caruthers thought he could smell last night's whiskey on his breath. The smell made him gag and almost drove him back, but looking over his shoulder, he saw that the damn closet door had swung open again even though he'd closed it earlier. It yawned and his office was now a closet and the closet was a sarcophagus with just enough room to open his mouth and scream.

Mike and Val backed out of the doorway as Mr. Caruthers stomped forward out of the office.

Despite the sweat on his forehead, he could breathe a little easier, and he mopped his brow with his shirt sleeve. Mike and Val traded glances. This was as much time as either had spent with their boss since their interviews in the Haimes's lobby. Mr. Caruthers wasn't looking too good.

"What do you expect to happen?" he asked. The open basement smelled musty as usual, but at least the walls were far enough away that they took a while to creep in.

Mike opened his mouth and gestured between him and Val, but no words came out.

"Well," Val said, picking up the slack. "At my last job, we worked in teams, someone moving stuff around while the other couple people cleaned. That's kind of how we work it now, but if there were three of us, it would go even faster. We'd get more done in less time."

Mr. Caruthers' eyes sparkled at the mention of that managerial wet dream. It was perfect timing, too. The security guard had just told him yesterday that Will Fredericks, the daytime building manager, was gunning for Mr. Caruthers.

Not to appear too eager, he grunted again. "I'll think about it. When Clarence shows up, I'll have a talk with him and we'll see what's what. But," he said, and fixed them both with one pointed finger, "if I catch you three racing around on your carts, you're all fired!"

In the moment of silence that followed, each pictured uptight Clarence, who seemed so keyed up he might have a heart attack if he had a little fun, careening around on a janitor cart, his blonde hair blown back, his eyes and mouth wide, tears and drool dribbling from all four corners. Mike and Val cracked up laughing; Mr. Caruthers only allowed himself a smile.

“Get out of here,” he said, looking back over his shoulder. His office had regained its normal proportions, which was good because he had paperwork to do. He turned his back on the ditzy duo, and went back into the office to wait for Clarence.

Mike and Val bumped fists, then went to the elevator. After a short wait, the doors opened, revealing Clarence. Mike and Val felt a rush of déjà vu.

Clarence smiled. He’d thoroughly cleaned the elevator’s walls on the ride down for the lobby.

“Excuse me,” he said, turning sideways and sliding past Mike and Val, trying to not breathe on them, as they boarded the elevator.

“Hey, Clarence,” Mike said. “Mr. Caruthers wants to talk with you.”

Clarence’s pale face turned white, and Mike blinked.

Val took a small step out of the elevator. “You okay, Clarence?”

“Clarence, you’re late,” Mr. Caruthers said, standing framed by the open doorway.

Turning, Clarence bowed his head and said, “Yes, sir.”

Frustrated by this simple confirmation, Mr.

Caruthers crossed his arms across his chest, resting them on his stomach. "Well?"

"I needed to fold my laundry, sir."

Laundry. Not a fake traffic jam. Not held up at another job. Not even the decency to claim that he'd overslept for a 6pm shift.

No. Laundry.

"Get in here."

Clarence followed meekly.

When he got into the office, Clarence held his breath and squeezed his elbows to his sides as he sidled past Mr. Caruthers to sit in the hard plastic chair on the far side of the desk. Mr. Caruthers sat, the chair creaking with his weight, and drummed his fingers on the desk top that Clarence wondered when it had last been cleaned.

"Clarence," he handed over a piece of triplicate paper, which Clarence took reluctantly. "I'm putting you on probation. You stayed late last night—"

"But sir—"

Mr. Caruthers slapped his palm on the desk. "I don't care!" There was dirt under his fingernails. He squared his shoulders, leaning forward. "I've told you time and again and you say you understand, but then you keep staying late. I take that to mean that you don't respect me or value your job. And now you're coming in late, and your excuse is that you needed to fold your laundry? Even Mike or Val wouldn't try to pull that one off, and they've come up with some doozies."

Something dawned in Mr. Caruthers eyes.

Clarence saw it and tensed, his one hand clenching at his thigh, the other crumpling one corner of the paper he held.

"Speaking of which..." Mr. Caruthers snatched the probation form from Clarence, who whined deep in his throat. His germs were crawling all over that paper, now in his boss's hands. "I'm making it a condition of your probation: you will be working with Mike and Val. The three of you will—"

The word stuck in his throat, but Clarence coughed it out. "No! No, sir, please. Don't make me work with them. I'll make them sick!"

Mr. Caruthers didn't even look up. "Don't be ridiculous. You haven't taken a sick day in—" he stopped writing, looking up. "Have you ever taken a sick day?"

"No, sir," Clarence said.

He grunted, nodding slightly. "Then I'm sure they don't have anything to worry about."

Mr. Caruthers slid the paper across the desk to Clarence, who signed where his boss pointed. Tearing out the yellow copy, Mr. Caruthers handed it to him. Clarence held it limply, his head hung. Looking up, tears shimmered in his pale blue eyes, magnified by his glasses. Mr. Caruthers swallowed the question that rose to his lips. He wasn't Clarence's friend; he was his boss and sympathy wasn't in the job description.

Mr. Caruthers scooted back, allowing a pathway between him and the desk, indicating that the conversation was over. Clarence rose, turned his back to his boss and, pulling out a Lysol wipe, cleaned the chair where he'd been sitting. Mr. Caruthers watched him with one eyebrow raised, but had worked with Clarence long enough that he wasn't surprised. Instead of throwing the wipe in the trash, Clarence wadded it up and stuffed it into his pocket. Then, he squeezed past Mr. Caruthers.

When Clarence reached the door, Mr. Caruthers said, "By midnight. Mike and Val usually start up on four and work their way down."

There were cobwebs in the corners of the office, a clean swath of use on an otherwise dust-covered desk and the air that Clarence breathed was thick with mold and mildew. Knowing that it was a lost cause, Clarence couldn't help saying over his shoulder, "You should wash your hands, sir. Fifty-four percent of viruses enter the body when we touch our face." Mr. Caruthers looked dumbstruck, so he said, "I don't want you to get sick either."

Mr. Caruthers looked at them, saw the dirt under his fingernails. Making sure that Clarence wasn't coming back, he started sucking at his fingertips. He couldn't stand the feeling of things digging under his nails.

Clarence rode the elevator up to the fifth floor where he retrieved his janitor's cart from the mechanical room. He wanted to ignore his probation and clean by himself, but he knew how hard it was to find a job right now. Besides, the people of the Haimes Building needed him, and he wouldn't abandon them.

Val saw him come out of the elevator on four and walked right over to him, getting uncomfortably close. Mike followed at a more sedate pace, although he had an eager expression on his face and he kept licking his lips. Clarence didn't like it. He dodged away from the elevator so he couldn't be trapped, keeping his janitor cart between him and them.

"Clarence, great!" Val beamed. Turning to Mike, she said, "See? Told you it was a good idea."

Mike grunted. He was trying to maneuver around Clarence's cart, but he wouldn't hold still. Val was trying to approach him from the other side, her smile wide. Mike wasn't going to let her beat him.

"Val, we should get back to it, you think?" Mike asked.

His brow smoothing, Clarence jumped in. "Yes. Mr. Caruthers told me I had to be done by midnight. I'm on probation," he answered their quizzical expressions.

"Oh, poor baby," Val pouted for him. She wanted to pat his shoulder, but he was out of reach. Instead, she put her hands on her hips. "Well, how we gonna do this?"

Twin blank looks. Val sighed. Men.

"Alright," she said. "Clarence and I will—"

"No, no," Mike cut her off. He stepped up to her, which allowed Clarence to scuttle away from them both. "I know what you're trying to do," he said, "and it ain't gonna work. We do this fair. No stacking the odds."

Clarence watched them whispering together and glancing at him. His stomach turned over and he was sweating again. He moved slowly, trying to not attract their attention, but the elevator button chimed when he pushed it and Mike and Val jumped like they'd forgotten he was there.

"This is stupid!" Val said more to Mike than Clarence. "Fine! Here's how it's gonna work: Clarence, Mike and I will move stuff around while you clean. Think you can handle that?"

Clarence thought it over. They'd be working ahead of him, so he could probably drag his feet at first to let them get a couple rooms ahead. Then, when they were far enough away that he didn't have to worry about them, he could relax and clean. Then, Mike and Val would come behind him and put everything back. Of course, they'd be dirtying the offices again, but at least they'd be safe from his germs, and he supposed that it was the best of a bad situation.

He'd have to move faster than he ever had before so he didn't let Mr. Caruthers down. Plus, he was now ostensibly cleaning the entire building. Everyone was counting on him.

"Yes," he said. Then, exceeding the number of words he'd ever said to either of them at one time, he said, "I think I can handle that."

Mike and Val looked at each other and started laughing. After a moment, Clarence realized that what he'd said, for whatever reason, had made them laugh. He was pleased that he'd made them laugh and he smiled, a little awkwardly.

After their laughter had died, the three of them stared at each other. Clarence said timidly, "You want to start up on the sixth? That way, we can clean our way down the building."

"Yar," Mike said, squinting an eye and hooking one finger into a pirate's claw, "genius! Lead the way, matey."

Having turned around, Clarence froze. The chrome door of the elevator faced him. His breath stopped in his throat and he flushed. He rubbed his hands against his thighs and bit his lip. Clarence didn't notice that she'd come up next to him until Val leaned around him and pushed the call button. Clarence jerked away, but tried to hide it by taking a stumbling step to his left.

The elevator hadn't moved and the door slid open with almost no hesitation. Mike and Val pushed forward, herding Clarence into the small car. He took a deep breath and stepped to the back, keeping his Dyson and cart between him and the other two janitors.

The car started rising, slowly. The number changed from 4 to 5. Val turned around to look at him, and Clarence tried to smile, pulling his lips tight and swaying back and forth to hide that he wasn't breathing. The number changed again as the pressure built in his closed throat, and he started feeling it behind his eyes. The car slowed and leveled itself with the floor while the edges of Clarence's vision started graying. The sound of the door grunting open drowned out his whine, his stifled need to exhale.

Mike and Val exited and Clarence allowed his lungs to deflate as quietly as he could, the blood rushing down from his brain, leaving him faint. Supporting himself on his cart, he followed.

The last time he'd allowed himself to be in an elevator with someone, it had been four years ago, his first year working in the Haimes building. He'd wanted to make a good first impression, so he'd arrived early and ridden up to the second floor with a woman who, smirking, had said she'd forgotten her briefcase. Clarence had made sympathetic sounds, but stood as far away as possible. Between the first and second floor, he'd coughed lightly. He'd really just cleared his throat, but then the woman had coughed, and Clarence's stomach had dropped. He'd spent the rest of the night assuring himself that it wasn't a big deal. The next day, Mr. Caruthers had told him that he could skip Sandra Leigh's office, she hadn't come in. Clarence had spent forty minutes cleaning her office from top to bottom, weeping the whole time, whispering fervent apologies.

Val started regretting their game to steal a five from Clarence in the first office on the sixth floor.

She and Mike moved some furniture around while Clarence stood frozen in the doorway. A smile on her face, she crossed the office toward Clarence, Mike hot on her heels. It was frustrating because it didn't seem like Clarence purposefully avoided them. He simply stepped around the opposite side of his cart and into the office. Val didn't want him to suspect something was up, so she stood in the doorway. Mike wanted to pursue Clarence, she could see it in the forward set of his shoulders and the way all of his weight was on his front foot, but he remained next to her.

Clarence stared at them blankly for a few moments before he said, “You can go ahead if you want. I’ll start cleaning in here.”

“Oh.” Val paused, trying to think of what to say. In a burst of inspiration, she said, “That’s okay. We don’t want you to think we’re ditching you.”

“Thank you, but that’s quite alright.”

At a loss, she nudged Mike, who said, “But we have to move the furniture back once you’re done.”

“I realize that,” Clarence said. His voice sounded weird, like he wasn’t breathing right or something. “But if you go ahead, I can clean, and then you just come behind me to put things back. I think that makes more sense, don’t you agree?”

He talked funny. Not an accent, but just the way he talked, like he was in a commercial or something. Son of a bitch, he was right, too.

“Fine,” Val said. “We’ll go ahead. Come on.”

Mike looked like he wanted to say something, but couldn’t pull the words together. Val spun on her heel and would’ve stomped from the room except she was trying to keep her poker face and she was wearing sneakers on carpet. Mike caught up to her at the next office, shaking her key in the lock and muttering.

“What the fuck, Val?”

“What the fuck what the fuck?”

“I mean, what the fuck?”

“You heard him!” She finally got the door unlocked. “It makes more sense this way.”

“Yeah but one of us could’ve stayed with him, you know, to help—”

"And have a chance to cheat? Nuh-uh. I don't care if it's you or me. I don't want to win like that and I for sure don't want to lose like that. Besides," she looked over her shoulder, "it's like he knows and he's just fucking with us. No," she cut off Mike, who had opened his mouth, "we play it cool. We'll get our chance."

Clarence breathed a sigh of relief, then shuddered. Mike and Val were too touchy-feely, always nudging each other, leaning in close to whisper something. They probably got each other sick all the time, a cold or the flu, or something even worse jumping back and forth between them. Well, he'd come behind them and clean up after them and everyone in the building would be a little healthier.

Once Mike and Val had done the light cleaning, they went to start moving furniture back. As they'd passed by the open doors, they'd glanced into each, expecting to see Clarence. They found him in the first office, leaning over the desk at an awkward angle, almost like he didn't know what to do with his body.

"Clarence, what are you doing?"

He jumped and almost lost his balance, knocking over a framed picture showing a smiling man, a smiling woman, a grinning dog and a grimacing teenager. Spinning, Clarence ducked his head, blushing, and pushed his glasses up on the bridge of his nose. They caught the fluorescent light and flashed.

"Cleaning," he murmured.

"Still?" Mike asked. He looked around; he and Val could've had this office cleaned in less than ten minutes and it had been more like forty-five. "We were just coming back to move stuff back." He checked his watch. "Jesus, it's after seven."

Clarence's head drooped further. "I'm sorry."

"It's okay, hon," Val said, playing the sympathetic mother to Mike's hard-assed father. She stepped forward while Clarence was distracted, his hands dangling at his sides. She almost regretted that it would be over so quickly. "Mike can go on ahead and do the light cleaning and you and I can trade off every other office. We can knock this—"

Clarence looked up as she was leaning closer to him, reaching out. He made a panicked noise and snatched his hands back behind him, scuttling away from Val as he did. His sudden movement startled her and she jumped back. Even Mike, standing at a little distance, his breath held in anticipation as Val went for the win, felt his heart skip a beat.

"What are you doing?" Clarence whined.

"What's wrong?" Val covered her disappointment with surprise.

Clarence had heard those words several times from his father, but the way Val had said them reminded him of one time when he'd been thirteen. He and his father had still been trying to get used to it just being the two of them. His father had asked him what was wrong, genuine concern an unfamiliar tone in his voice, while Clarence stared at their front door. He'd just come in and thought he should clean the knob he'd just touched. Some deep instinct had told Clarence that he couldn't tell his dad what he was thinking, that he wouldn't understand.

"Nothing," Clarence said to Val, as he'd said to his father so many times as the concern turned to obligation over the years.

"Alright," Mike said from the doorway, "well, I guess I'll go down to five and start the light cleaning."

"Okay. Clarence and I will finish up here. Okay, Clarence?" Val asked tenderly, even though she was getting a little frustrated.

Clarence nodded and pushed his glasses up on his nose, which slid back down immediately.

By nine-thirty, which was when they usually took their dinner break, Val was well on her way to being pissed. Mike, too, became more sarcastic with both of them, Val especially. They were only down to the third, with only two hours to go. It was next to impossible how slowly Clarence cleaned. Mike was doing all the light cleaning and moving the furniture. Val was cleaning three out of every four offices, but she thought she'd seen Clarence coming out of one of the offices she'd done, his expression somewhere between guilty and satisfied.

While Clarence washed the plastic tray of his Healthy Choice dinner, Mr. Caruthers came into the break room. "How's he doing?"

"He's awesome," Mike said. "Funny, great with kids, an all-around good guy. In fact—" He paused. "I think I'm falling for him."

Mouth pulled into a tight line, Mr. Caruthers turned to Val, who didn't think it was funny either.

"Slow. Mike's doing the light stuff and

Clarence and I are cleaning offices, but he moves so slow," she said, drawing the last two words out. "We'll be lucky to get everything done by midnight."

"You will," Mr. Caruthers said pointedly to both of them, stating a fact, not offering encouragement.

However, he was quite satisfied. Somehow, he had killed three birds with one stone. These two would make sure that Clarence got his work done, and Clarence was just the wet blanket to keep the ditzy duo under control. Mr. Caruthers went back to his office, convinced that he'd made a brilliant managerial decision and that it wasn't just a happy accident.

The lobby's entrance had three-quarter windows which, at night, showed a beautiful view of the dark sky and the brightly-lit parking lot. It was four past midnight and Mike was moving furniture back into place while Val coiled up the cord of her vacuum. Clarence was in the women's bathroom. He'd been in there for close to half an hour, had been in the men's for forty minutes before that. Mike slid the last chair into place, then straightened, rubbing at his lower back.

"I've," he sang, "had the time of my life. And I owe it all to you." He jabbed his middle finger in the direction of the bathrooms.

"Knock it off," Val said.

"Whatever." Mike pouted, putting cleaning supplies back on their cart.

Reading his mind, Val said, "No one said this was going to be easy. That was the point, remember?"

"Yeah, but this isn't even fun." He paused. "I

say we go to Mr. Caruthers tomorrow and tell him Clarence sucks and he's on his own."

Val cocked an eyebrow, smirking. "You forfeiting?"

"No!" Mike said. His face pinched in thought. Conclusively, he said, "No, you're not gonna win that easily."

Val opened her mouth, but then Clarence walked out of the women's restroom, pausing to wipe off the door handle. He pushed his cart ahead of him as he crossed the lobby. Val's mouth hung open, like she was in the middle of saying something, but as he drew closer, she closed it, leaning back on her left foot and crossing her arms. Mike's eyebrows were lowered and he held a bottle of glass cleaner and a filthy rag. Clarence would have been disgusted, but he was too elated to notice. He stopped in front of them and blinked tears out of his eyes.

"Thank you," he whispered. Louder, afraid they hadn't heard him, he repeated himself.

"For what?"

Val shot Mike a dirty look, then asked, "For what, hon?"

Clarence drew a deep breath. "It's hard to explain. I just wanted to thank you for helping me get my work done. Mr. Caruthers will be proud of us." After another deep, hitching breath, he said, "Goodnight."

He turned to leave. Mike and Val looked at each other, speechless. Across the lobby, Clarence had called the elevator and cleaned the button. When it chimed, Val jumped forward.

"You're not going home already?" she asked, an idea making her voice cheerful.

Clarence allowed himself to be stopped by her voice. His heart thudded in his chest, from fear or excitement, he couldn't tell.

The last time he'd had a friend was his sophomore year in high school. High school was a disgusting place where germs flourished in group showers after gym, the cafeteria where the air was hot and thick, and classrooms, thirty-person incubators good for nothing but the spread of disease. Her name had been Lisa and she'd worn all black and a spiked dog-collar. She'd tried to convince Clarence that everyone died eventually and even though there wasn't a heaven, he could at least take comfort in the fact that consciousness was just random bursts of electricity no one fully understood and therefore couldn't substantially explain the difference between a live person and a dead one. But at least she didn't want to be touched either, and that was something he could understand perfectly.

The elevator door slid shut in front of him and Clarence turned. Val stopped a few feet away, Mike following more sedately.

"We're going to the bar. Wanna come?"

Fear overpowered excitement and Clarence shivered. Luckily, he had his excuse ready. "Sorry, but I'm filthy. I need to go home and take a shower."

"Tomorrow night," Mike said, joining the conversation.

"Yeah," Val chimed in. "We got the day off, so we can get there for specials."

The cold sweat on Clarence's body made him shudder. He flexed his hands at his sides, rubbing his palms on his thighs. "I'll have to see. I might be busy."

"Alright, cool," Val said, still cheerful. She took her cell phone out of her pocket and flipped it open. "What's your number?" Clarence recited it for her, excitement fluttering his stomach. "I'll text you when we're heading out."

"Oh," Clarence said. "I don't have a cell phone. That's my home number."

"Oh," Val said, like the idea of using a phone to call someone was a little weird. "Well, I'll call you then."

"Okay," Clarence said. Mike and Val didn't move, so he said, "Cool," the word unfamiliar in his mouth.

Mike and Val laughed and slapped high fives and Clarence cringed, pushing the elevator call button.

After the car had opened and he'd stepped inside, he gestured at his cart. "Sorry, there's not enough room for all three of us. You'll call me tomorrow?"

"For sure," Mike said, giving him a thumbs up.

As the door closed, Clarence gave them a little wave, smiling.

Then, turning to Mike, Val said, "To be continued!"

5

Richard stood in his kitchen, an open bottle of Jack Daniels on the counter in front of him. He could smell it, he realized, his mouth watering. But his lawyers had advised him that he shouldn't appear to be hungover in court tomorrow, so he capped the bottle and put it in the cupboard.

Now he didn't know what to do with himself. He puttered around the apartment, specifically not going into the kitchen. He got a cup of water from the bathroom and looked at the TV, but then he got up and checked the bathtub, to make sure that it was empty. While he was in there, he decided to brush his teeth, but forgot mouthwash.

Richard changed into his pajamas, watched some more TV, feeling trapped in the apartment, but he didn't have anywhere to go. The bottle of Jack waited inside the cupboard, half-full and always the optimist. Richard drank more water.

In the hospital, with all the slashes and stab wounds stitched and healing, he'd surfed the ocean of semi-consciousness on the best drugs that insurance could buy. After being released, his doctor, a family friend, had prescribed double the usual prescription of Oxycontin. Richard had then been able to stretch them out by only taking them at night, when the discomfort prevented him from sleeping.

His parents, ashamed by the rumors circulating about their son and his family, were even more embarrassed that their son was turning into a druggie.

"No," his father had said when Richard called, his scars itching almost as if they missed the knife that caused them. "You don't need drugs. My leg looks like goddamn pegboard from Korea and the most I ever took was aspirin."

"But Dad," he'd whined, his middle-aged voice cracking with pubescent supplication. Victoria had hated that about him. He hated it about himself, but he couldn't help it. "I need it. You don't understand."

"Don't understand, huh?" His father's voice had dropped twenty degrees. "Why don't you try being a man for once in your miserable life, Richard," and hung up on him.

Richard had had a few pills left and tried to wean himself so he wouldn't need to go cold turkey. Chill turkey was just as bad and he awoke those mornings feeling like he hadn't slept at all, his mind a gray fog. Two months after getting out of the hospital, he went to bed drug-free for the first time.

After thirty-two minutes of staring at the ceiling, he'd gotten up and gone to the kitchen, poured himself a shot of Jack. The warmth had spread through his stomach, making his limbs feel looser. The cold sweat on his body had warmed as his blood vessels dilated and he took another shot, so the first one wouldn't get lonely. He'd chuckled on his way to bed, flopped down and fell right asleep.

It had been three months since he'd gone to bed

sober, he thought. He was tired but not sleepy and wondered when the last time he'd made that distinction was. His whole body ached with fatigue, his scars itching like mad. It was almost one in the morning and he needed to be in court by nine. Richard drank the last of the water and returned the cup to the bathroom on his way to the bedroom.

The bathtub was still empty.

Richard turned on his lamp and settled into bed. Swearing, he got back up, went to the living room to get the book he was reading. Getting under the covers again, he fidgeted to get comfortable, then started reading. But he couldn't concentrate. The words looked like they were written in another language. He'd never stopped to think how weird the word 'the' looked, and it was everywhere.

Richard put his book down and shut the lamp off. He'd had this bed for five months but it already sagged in a groove shaped to his usual sleeping position. Except he didn't feel like lying on his side yet, so he moved around, still unable to get comfortable.

Finally, he just made himself lie still. His eyes had gotten used to the dark and he stared at the ceiling. His eyes slipped shut, and the darkness threaded with lines of light that pulsed with his heartbeat. Then, the black brightened to gray and receded.

Richard was in a high school gym. Not his high school in Grosse Pointe, but a different one. Maple leaves decorated the walls. The music was too loud and it scared him. He'd never been to a dance before, but his friend, Matt, had insisted. Matt's girlfriend had a friend and Matt had promised that he'd bring a friend for her.

He stood, holding a cup of Pepsi, on the edge of the crowd. Matt and his girlfriend, Lila, had deserted him to dance and were grinding their pelvis together somewhere in the middle of crowd, trying to hide from the chaperones. Richard's gut twisted with both envy and confusion. Everyone always asked him why he didn't have a girlfriend. He knew that he should have one, but girls scared him a little.

He took a sip of Pepsi, not seeing his middle-aged hand, hair and gnarly tendons standing out on the back of it. Matt and Lila had only seen their friend, not the man he'd grown into, a scar dimpling his left cheek. Before dragging Matt off to the dance floor, Lila had assured Richard that he'd be fine, her friend would know him, she'd shown her a picture from Matt's yearbook.

"My hair looked stupid," Richard had whined, unheard over the music.

It didn't matter, they'd already walked away. He had nothing to do but wait.

Standing there, watching the bouncing and jerking dancers, he felt something that he didn't remember, his stomach dropping with the unfamiliarity. He itched all over. Like when he'd had chicken pox and every movement was tingling torture as the sores on his skin stretched and contracted, rubbing against his clothing.

Something was coming. Blinding pain shot

through his shoulder and the red lights above the DJ were his blood, the strobing light, the flash of the knife. He felt her, coming closer. He wanted to drop the plastic cup and hunch his shoulders in, put his hands to his face, hide, but he didn't move.

His dream of his memory held him prisoner and he stood there dumbly, holding a cup of lukewarm Pepsi that made his mouth taste like shit and he wished he'd brought some Altoids so he could be curiously strong and he knew she was coming, could feel it in the scars that dotted his body.

She'd laid a hand on his arm, almost making him drop his pop and he'd turned, blushing. She'd smiled thinly and he'd relaxed a little, even though he tried to not breathe directly into her face for the rest of the night.

That's what had happened. That wasn't what happened now.

He turned because in his memory, he felt her hand on his arm, but Victoria was still a few feet away. The skin on her left arm was streaked crimson and hung in flaps, severed veins dangling like vines. Her black hair was wet and plastered flat against her skull which jutted in sharp angles. The corners of her mouth turned down as her lips widened in a smile.

"We miss you…"

The people at the dance had evaporated like the faded memories they were. It was just the two of them now, the doors too far away, padlocked, the windows shuttered and too high up. As she shuffled forward, her arms stretched, snaking toward him, bending at unnatural angles.

Richard turned away from her to run, but stopped. A bathtub sat in the corner. He could see Lucy's hair, fanned out and floating in the water.

Richard screamed, thrashing out of bed and falling to the floor. Lying there, his head and heart pounded. He jumped up, ran to the bathroom, turned on the light. He squinted in the sudden brightness and pushed back the shower curtain.

The bathtub was empty.

Richard sat on the floor, his hands and legs shaking. After a while, he was able to stand and walk to the kitchen. The Jack was waiting in the cupboard.

"Fuck you," he said to the lawyers, at home and probably asleep, and drank straight from the bottle.

Friday

6

Clarence took a deep breath and pushed open the door to the bar. He walked in without pausing to clean the door's handle.

"You should clean that," he scolded.

"It doesn't matter," he answered. "I have friends now."

He brushed up against people, giving little apologetic smirks to them. It was crowded, more so than movies and TV shows had always made it seem. Loud techno music thumped a heartbeat and people danced or just swiveled their hips in place, holding their drinks and shouting into each other's faces. Clarence craned his neck this way and that, then he saw Val waving to him. There seemed to be more people than when he'd first walked in and for every person he squeezed past, every group he pushed through, never losing his sycophantic smile, Mike and Val didn't seem to get any closer.

Motion catching his eye, a woman had needed to stop dancing because of a sneezing fit. Concerned, Clarence changed course, putting his arms out to part the thickening press of bodies between him and the woman. The woman wasn't covering her mouth as she sneezed, and he wanted to tell her that she should. A sneeze could propel germs up to twenty feet at a hundred miles an hour.

As he came up to her, blood began to spray from her nose, misting those closest to her, who didn't seem to notice. Clarence covered his face, feeling the warm droplets bead in the hair on the backs of his hands.

The woman was sneezing and coughing violently now, each spasm twisting her back, the blood running down her face, staining her white hospital gown scarlet. Clarence reached out and touched her shoulder. She straightened up. Blood covered the lower half of a face well known, much loved.

"Clarence," his mother said. "Look what you've done."

The techno thump turned into a monotonous, high-pitched tone. Clarence snatched his hand away, pressing his palms flat on his thighs, not catching his mother as she fell to the floor.

Everyone stopped dancing and stood, staring at Clarence. Then, one by one, they all fell, dead.

Clarence looked down at himself. His shroud billowed around him in the wind of exhaled, dying breaths. His face felt hot, flushed, but his hands were cold, clammy.

Nearby loomed an ebony clock and it gonged twelve times with deep-throated finality. Then it said, "And the Red Death held illimitable dominion over all."

The thump of the thick, hard-cover book falling to the floor next to his bed woke Clarence. Sitting up in bed, heart hammering, bathed in a cold sweat, one thought filled his mind: he couldn’t go out with Mike and Val.

7

Clarence didn't know what time he'd woken up from his nightmare, but he'd been cleaning ever since. His eyes burned with fatigue and the fumes of ammonia. As the windows lightened with the coming dawn, sounds drifted through the ceiling from the apartment upstairs.

First, an alarm clock, loud in the stillness, buzzed from the second bedroom. It stopped, then the unsteady sound of footsteps, the mother, rambled out into the hallway and into the larger bedroom. Muffled words, then she went to the kitchen. Back in the bedroom, more muffled words were followed by a shocked moment of silence. The younger of the children started crying, high and loud. Running from the kitchen, the mother yelled at the older, who went into the bathroom and slammed the door.

The younger's crying tapered off, whether by soothing or accusation, Clarence didn't know, though he'd heard both before. Either way, Clarence judged it to be safe to start vacuuming.

It had been his father's rule, back when Clarence had wanted to do such things as go see his friends and play at the neighborhood park: don't be the first one to break the silence. Clarence often woke up early. So on Saturday mornings, he would get up, get a bowl of cereal and turn on cartoons, turning down the volume so low that he had to sit practically in front of the TV to hear anything at all, eating quietly during commercials. Around ten, his father would get up, but still not allow Clarence to go to the park or any of his friends' houses. Eventually, he stopped asking, which suited his father just fine.

Clarence started vacuuming in his bedroom, working out into the hallway, the second bedroom, a brief stop in the bathroom to get the corners, out into the living room, corners of the kitchen and dining room, finishing up by the little linoleum area near the front door, where he returned the vacuum to the closet.

After putting it away, he stood, fists on his hips, light sweat drying on his back, nodding in appreciation and approval of his clean apartment. Overhead, the children chased each other, the stomping sounding like it would cave in the ceiling. But Clarence was in a good mood and paid it no mind, intent on getting into the shower and getting himself clean.

In the shower, he thought about Mike and Val's invitation for about the thousandth time since getting up. It was silly. Going out was silly. Everything he needed was right here. He had his books and the internet. Sure he went out for groceries and stuff like that, but that was different. He didn't need to go out for company.

The scalding water briefly drove all thought from Clarence's head while he rinsed. Shutting off the shower, he grabbed a fresh towel and stepped out. He stood, looking back at the drain for a moment. Then, he shook his head and started drying off.

It was nothing, not important. Just something that he thought had happened.

After cleaning the shower and dressing, he turned on the news and sat on the couch, his feet up on the ottoman. The last U.S. troops were leaving Iraq.

Irrelevant. They were coming home just to be sent somewhere else, probably Afghanistan, maybe Iran or North Korea. There was always some war going on somewhere.

Click.

The stock market was still reeling from Congress waiting until the last minute to approve raising the debt ceiling.

Big surprise. Congress was always disagreeing about something. Things would smooth out and the average American's life wouldn't change all that much.

Click.

The screen showed footage that Clarence recognized: Asian men with sterile masks over their faces holding bundles of dead chickens by their feet. Clarence fumbled with the remote, turning up the volume. The picture on the screen cut to more stock footage of a man in a white clean-suit hunched over a microscope.

"—wasn't sure what details would be published, but the scientists involved assured us that the details of their methodology wouldn't be part of the article. As you may remember, H5N1, more commonly known as Avian Flu, is communicable only through direct contact with carriers of the disease, but now virologists at Ohio University have said that they have successfully mutated the germ to live for longer periods of time in the air."

The anchor turned to her partner and said, "The controversial article is set to be published in next month's Scientific American, although it's likely there will be pressure from the Center for Disease Control and Homeland Security for approval of the article's contents before publication."

The other anchor looked grim. "Truly a chilling possibility." Turning, he said, brighter now with a new camera angle, "Justin Verlander accepted the league MVP today—"

Clarence muted the TV, the remote slipping out of his trembling hands. Walking on shaking legs, he went into his office, woke up his computer, went to the CDC's website. It was rare for the virus to jump from poultry to humans, but IT happened, and when it did, its mortality rate was about sixty percent. Its spread was slow, which had allowed outbreaks to be contained rather easily, happening only through close and prolonged contact.

Clarence went to the bathroom to wash his hands. Coming back into the office, he regarded his computer, keyboard, and mouse with suspicion. He air-dusted the keyboard and air vents on the monitor, scrubbed everything with Lysol Multi-Surface, and went to wash his hands again. Sitting back down at the computer, he took a moment to breathe the fresh, clean air before he wondered how long the air would stay clean.

Searching for information about the article, Clarence found an iteration that the spread of H5N1 was slow, because of the necessity of close contact to spread. The OU scientists wanted to know what mutations were necessary, if it was even possible, for H5N1 to be able to sustain long periods of time in the air, making it more easily communicable between people. The scientists claimed to be working in the public's best interest.

Clarence sat back in his desk chair, pulling his glasses from his face and pinching the bridge of his nose.

Yeah, so were the scientists at the Manhattan Project. The ones who developed Agent Orange. Weaponized anthrax.

Clarence couldn't read anymore. Of this anyway. He needed to relax. His recliner on the other side of the room called to him, *The Andromeda Strain* by Michael Crichton on one of the overstuffed arms. He'd read for a couple hours, then make some lunch. By then, it would surely be after noon and Val would feel safe calling him.

His heart beat a little harder at the thought. Going out. Meeting up with people who'd be happy to see him, buy him a beer, maybe slap him five, like Mike and Val did all the time. Clarence shuddered, but still felt thrilled. Like in the dream, knowing that he was infecting everyone, but at the same time, not caring.

He sprayed Lysol on the keyboard and mouse, then went to bathroom to wash his hands. Crossing the hallway, he glanced at the TV, which he'd left on. He stopped, one foot on the tile floor of the bathroom, one foot on the carpet of the hallway, and leaned back to see the TV.

A little girl, blonde, pigtails, was reaching for the pump of the soap dispenser in an otherwise clean, white kitchen. The mother stood in the background, obliviously putting groceries away while amoeba-like, grotesquely colored things crawled on the plastic pump that the girl was reaching for in slow motion like a death scene in a movie.

Clarence took three running steps into the living room, fumbled with the remote, managed to get the sound on.

"—on your soap dispenser pump." The mother onscreen turned just in time to grab the little girl's hand before it reached its germ-covered goal. The mother chided her daughter with a smile and a shake of her head and reached into one of the grocery bags, pulling out a Lysol Hands-Free Soap Dispenser, unpackaged and ready. The little girl waved her hand under the spout, which dribbled soap to her giggled delight. "Lysol. Disinfect to protect."

Clarence turned the TV off. He turned in a slow circle to face the kitchen. The soap dispenser stood next to the sink, a false friend waiting to get him sick. He sprang into the kitchen, knocked it from the counter into the sink and turned on the water, waiting for it to steam. Then, he took the Comet Bleach from under the sink, a steel wool pad and started scrubbing it, ignoring the burning pain in his hands.

After about a minute, he couldn't stand to have his hands under the water anymore and dropped the soap dispenser, cradling them to his chest. After the burning sensation subsided, he turned off the water, retrieved the dispenser and set it back on the counter.

Stared at it.

Imagined the germs crawling on it. Getting onto his hands.

Entering his body. Making him sick. Spreading.

The steam from the hot water had condensed on the wall over the sink. Droplets of water puddled where it sat on the counter. Waiting. Cleaning it wasn't good enough. Not for him, not for anyone else.

Clarence whirled, grabbed his keys on the way out the door.

It was only a two minute drive from the Applewood Apartments to the CVS on Grand River. Two of the longest minutes of Clarence's life.

He parked at the back of the lot, away from all the other cars. Getting out, he started walking across the parking lot before realizing that he hadn't cleaned the interior or the door handle. He stopped, turned back, then stopped again. He still hadn't washed his hands after using the computer. He used the sanitizer from his pocket. But it wasn't good enough. There had been studies done, using sanitizer versus washing, and washing got rid of twenty-two percent more germs because the germs were actually removed from the skin instead of dying and rotting, providing fodder for other germs. He needed to wash his hands, and soon. He parked far enough away from the other cars in the parking lot that no one should need to come anywhere near his car.

But if someone stole his car…

That poor, unfortunate person would get into a cesspool of Clarence's germs, probably get sick, and sicker, and sickest until he died, but not before he went home to his family, went out with his friends—

Quick, Clarence thought, sprinting back to his car. He scrubbed, wiped, vacuumed, finally closing the door, wiping off the handle and ran toward the store to make up for lost time.

Aisle after aisle, he held his breath, twisted his body to avoid brushing up against people, the store strangely crowded for a Friday mid-morning. The dispensers weren't with the soap, and Clarence ran a nervous hand through his hair. Freezing, he sensed something just in time to drop his shoulder and step away from the manager, who had come up behind him.

The manager, a tall, spindly man with a long face, stepped back in surprise. "I'm sorry, I didn't mean to startle you. Can I help you find something?"

Clarence tried to speak without breathing out too much. "Lysol Hands-Free Soap Dispenser."

"Ah," the manager said, smiling. A gold tooth flashed from way back in his mouth. The manager led Clarence, who lagged behind at a safe distance, to another aisle. He took a box off a lower shelf and handed it to Clarence. "Here you go. Last one."

Clarence stammered, then said, "No. I need three. At least. Five if you have them."

The manager just looked at him, eyes and lips

thin like the rest of him. "I'm sorry sir, but we only have the one left."

"Can you check in the back? Maybe you have some left in the back that you could give me because I really need at least three. Five, if you have them."

"I will definitely check, sir. Why don't you finish your shopping, and I'll find what I can and meet you at the register."

Clarence missed the manager's placating tone, nodded, and bustled away to the front, waiting by the Kodak kiosk.

Eventually, the manager emerged from the small storeroom, only one box under his arm. He strode to the front of the store, handing the box to Clarence, who took it, dumbfounded.

"I told you. I need three. At least."

"Yes, sir," the manager said, an edge to his voice now. "But we only had one in the back. And I had to scrounge around for it." His upper lip lifted in a sneer. "It wasn't where it was supposed to be."

"But—somewhere else. If this—this one wasn't where it was supposed to be—are you telling me that it's completely out of the realm of possibility—"

"Sir—"

"—that there isn't another one somewhere else?" Clarence clutched the boxes to his chest, crushing them into each other. "Can you please go check, please?" He looked down at his hands. "And hurry, please."

"Sir," the manager said, keeping his voice even. "I can assure you, I looked everywhere. Now," he took a slight step forward, causing Clarence to step back, "I'd like you to please calm down. You're making the other customers nervous."

Clarence glanced around. The girl behind the counter quickly looked back down at her register, but the man who was buying a newspaper and a gallon of milk stared at him.

There was something like his father in the manager, an instant assertion of dominance that left Clarence cringing. "I'm sorry," he mumbled. "Is there any way—"

"Sir," the manager said, flashing a look over to the cashier, who nonchalantly picked up the phone, "I'd like you to pay for your purchases now."

Clarence nodded.

"Have a nice day," he said, "and thank you for shopping at CVS."

Clarence went up to the cashier, who stood with one fist on her hip, one hand outstretched, smacking her gum.

"Uh," he fumbled with the boxes, feeling the manager's gaze on his back. He held the boxes out, barcodes pointing toward the woman. "Can you scan them without touching them, please?"

She rolled her eyes and picked up the scanning gun. It beeped twice, and she tapped a key. "Total is forty-two forty."

Clarence nodded, got out his wallet, a credit card, and the packet of wipes from another pocket. The cashier rolled her eyes again, blew a bubble and popped it as Clarence cleaned his card before swiping it, using the corner to tap the screen. He signed, using a new wipe to clean the pen, then shook his head when the cashier offered him a bag. The manager's glare escorted him out the door.

Back at his apartment, Clarence dismantled the boxes and other packaging. He put one next to the sink in the kitchen, then went to the bathroom to set the other one up. The soap cartridge clicked into place, the battery door snapped shut and Clarence set it on the counter, breathing slowly to calm his racing heart. Turning on the faucet, he tentatively waved his hand under the spout.

He giggled a little when the soap came out, the machine whirring. He rubbed his hands together vigorously under the water, waved for more soap, washed, waved, laughed at the sound. He was four years old again, when his mother used to send him back into the bathroom when he didn't wash his hands, until he discovered how fun it was to push the pump down and watch the soap come out, some clear, some like milk, some yellow, his favorite color.

He was still laughing, but crying too, as he felt the strength running out of his legs. He knelt, leaning against the cabinet, sobbing, the rushing sound of water going down the drain loud in his ears, growing louder, until he stopped crying, stood up, turned off the faucet.

The water wasn't draining. The stopper was up. Unbelieving, he pulled the lever. The stopper dropped. He pushed it back in and the stopper rose, but still didn't drain. Impossible. Clarence put a bottle of

Drano down each drain every month. He stepped over, reached around the toilet and grabbed the plunger. With a soft gurgle, the water started emptying.

"What are you doing?"

Clarence looked around, but he was alone in the bathroom. The voice had reminded him of his mother, but what he imagined her voice would've sounded like as a little girl. He put the plunger back, pulled the stopper from the sink, then peered down it as if it were possible to actually see the problem.

"I said, what are you doing?"

"Oh," Clarence said, starting up and looking around. Now, he recognized the voice coming from the shower drain, "it's you." He replaced the stopper. "I was just, uh—washing my hands."

"Oh. Okay."

Clarence leaned over the tub. "I thought you'd left for school. Not feeling well?"

"I told you," said the little girl. "I don't go to school. Mommy won't let me."

Clarence wasn't sure what to say. After a moment, he said, "I think there's some kind of law about that." The little girl didn't answer. "So—you're feeling alright, then?"

"Okay, I guess." The girl's voice was low, hard to hear. "Sad. I guess."

"Oh, I'm sorry," Clarence said, sympathetic to the tone of the girl's voice, small, unhappy. "Why are you sad?"

"Mommy makes me do chores all day while she cries." Her words came slowly, like it was the first time the girl had stopped to think about why she was sad. “I don’t like doing chores. And I don’t like it when Mommy cries. She doesn’t like me when she cries. That’s why she makes me clean.”

“Oh,” Clarence perked up. “I’m sure that’s not true. You know,” he leaned closer to the drain, “I could hear you this morning, when your older—brother?—hit you. It sounded like your mom—”

“I don’t have any brothers.”

“Oh. Sister?”

“No.”

“Oh.” The pipe must go to another apartment other than the one over his. “Well, anyway, I’m sure your mother likes you just fine. Oh!” he exclaimed, remembering. “Just because she makes you clean doesn’t mean that she doesn’t like you. My mother taught me that being clean is very important and it’s the best thing she ever taught me.” He stopped, thinking, remembering his mother, the lessons she taught him and their price.

“Did she ever… hug you?”

Clarence sat back in surprise, his shoulders stiff from supporting his weight. “Yes. Of course.”

“Mommy never hugs me. SpongeBob hugs Patrick when he’s sad ‘cause they’re friends. She doesn’t like me,” she said, with finality.

Clarence made some sound, incapable for the moment of words, thinking about his father, who had hugged him after Clarence had won second place in the Pinewood Derby when he’d been nine. “What about your dad?”

"He's not here," she said. "Mommy goes out to look for him every day, but always comes back without him and gets mad at me."

Clarence sat up, stretched his back. The poor girl seemed to not have anyone, an unloving mother, like his father, no father of her own, couldn't go to school—

"Do you have any friends, other children?"

"No. They play outside around the tree, but Mommy won't let me go out and play with them."

"That doesn't sound very fair."

"That's what I said!"

There was a defiant tone to her voice that worried Clarence. Parents were supposed to be obeyed. But the girl sounded so lonely.

Suddenly excited, Clarence leaned forward and said directly into the drain. "Do you have a teddy bear?"

"A duck," she said, a little guarded now.

"What's his name?"

"Ducky."

"That makes sense." He paused, cautious. "Do you ever hug Ducky?"

"I kiss him every night," she said. "But he never turns into a prince."

"Well, I want you to hug Ducky, and when you hug Ducky, think of me giving you a hug, because I'm your friend now, and I don't want you to be sad anymore."

The little girl was silent for so long that Clarence got scared, feeling dirty, wrong. He didn't know the little girl, didn't want her to think he was some kind of creep, tell her mother and then call the police.

"Okay," the little girl said, her voice a little stronger now. "What's your name?"

"Oh! Clarence," he said. He searched his memory from their conversation from a couple nights ago, when she told him a fairy tale version of her life. "Your name is... Lucy?"

"Yes," she said, "Princess Lucy."

"Oh my goodness," he exclaimed, warming up to the game. "Please forgive me, Princess Lucy. By your leave, m'lady." He bowed, ridiculous because he was leaning over the lip of the tub, but happy when the little girl giggled.

"Of course, fair Clarence," she said, laughter still in her voice. "I forgive you. And I'll think of you whenever I hug Ducky."

Clarence chuckled, then just sat there, having run out of ways to contribute to the game.

Lucy was silent for a time as well. Then, she said, "You're funny. Do you play this good with your other friends?"

Clarence thought of Mike and Val, thought of them high-fiving each other while he watched. They were always playing games. They raced down the halls, wrestled with each other when a door needed to be unlocked, held their breath in the elevator, tried to see which one could stuff more of their dinner into their mouths at once. He was afraid, watching them touch each other, touch each other's food, wrestle and lick their palms before slapping five, but excited, too.

He thought about Mickey, his best friend growing up, playing at the park, after waiting, watching at the window for Mickey to show up, how they played, tackled each other, spit in their palms and rubbed them together, swearing allegiance to each other as spit brothers, forever.

It was a miracle Mickey had survived being his friend.

"No," he said. "I guess not."

"Oh." She sounded disappointed. "What do you and your friends do?"

Clarence stuttered. "Well, uh—I don't really—I mean, my friends and I, we don't…" Then, a light went on in Clarence's brain. "Oh! These two people I work with, Mike and Val, they invited me out to a bar tonight—that's like a place grown-ups go, kind of like a playground, I guess—but I don't know if I'm going to go."

"Why not?" Her voice cracked with shock.

That struck Clarence speechless for a moment before he blurted, "Because! They could get sick—if I touched them, they could get—"

"Does your tummy hurt?"

"No."

"Too hot?"

"No, but—"

"Cold?"

"No, I'm fine, I guess."

"One time, I got the chicken pox and I itched all over. Do you have the chicken pox?"

"No. I feel fine."

Lucy stopped babbling, her silence painful to listen to. "I'm sorry. Just trying to help."

"I know, I'm sorry."

She continued, as if she hadn't heard him, "If you're not feeling sick, how are you going to get them sick?"

Clarence thought about how to answer her, how much to tell her, if it would scare her.

"One time," he said, his words slow, "when I was a kid—you're what, six, seven?"

"I'm eight," she said, and Clarence could picture her with her fists on her hips, glaring up at him.

Except he was talking to her through a drain. Somehow, that made what he had to confess easier.

"I was eleven—I got sick. My mom always took care of me when I got sick. But," and he stopped, squeezed his eyes shut. Then, he took a deep, shaky breath. "Mom got sick. She was so busy taking care of me, she didn't—have the—didn't take care of… And she…"

Lucy's voice was tiny when she asked, "Did she die?"

The words were too small, unable to encompass everything that had happened. The hospital, the crying, the masks he and his father had worn to visit his mother. The coughing, the droplets of blood that stained the sheets. The way she squeezed his hand, coughing, coughing, not breathing in. The high-pitched screaming of the machines in her room as people came running in and his father pulled him out, yanking him away from his mother who was squeezing his hand so tight it felt like it would break, that his arm would pull out of his socket because she wasn't letting go.

"Yes, she died."

They fell silent.

Finally, Lucy said, "If I had friends who wanted to play with me, I would go out, even if I was sick. The only way I'd stay inside is if I was throwing up or something."

Clarence thought about it. "I guess," he said, remembering his dream from last night.

"Everyone needs friends to play with," she said, absolute conviction in her voice. "Playing by yourself gets so-o bo-oring."

His heart started thumping at the thought. "You know what? You're right! You're absolutely right."

"Yeah!" she exclaimed, her voice high with delight. "You should go out and play with them! It'll be fun!"

"Yeah!" Clarence stood up, caught up in the moment, wanting to call them right now before he had a chance to change his mind. Then, he remembered that Val was supposed to call him. Kneeling back down by the tub, he lowered his voice, as if scared that his father might hear him and give him a spanking. "You know what you should do, though? You should do all your chores extra good today, so maybe your mother will let you go out and play." When she didn't answer right away, he cleared his throat, unsure of himself. "You know, with the kids that play around the tree?"

The silence stretched on, until Clarence sat back, puzzled.

8

Princess Lucy sat cross-legged on the floor in the living room watching her favorite episode of SpongeBob SquarePants, which was just ending. The little girl, brushing the black hair out of her face, closed her eyes and whispered a magic chant, thinking of her favorite moment in the episode when Mr. Krabs turns into a talking Krabby Patty and SpongeBob runs screaming from the restaurant. When the theme song started, she opened her eyes, smiling.

Behind her, from the bathroom, came a high-pitched shriek, her mother's voice cracking.

Lucy whirled toward the sound, the picture on the TV changing to show her mother's face, blurry as if seen through water or broken glass. Lucy's hands, small with her father's stubby fingers, reached up toward her mother, trying to push her away. Then, the screen went dark.

Lucy jumped up, looking around. The couch! She pulled the coffee table out of the way and squeezed herself underneath, trying to hold her breath so her mother wouldn't hear her. Soon, the queen would leave again, and she could go back to watching cartoons, or maybe play in her room. She wanted to run away, but her mother's magic had destroyed the outside world. Outside was nothing but gray fog.

Victoria stormed into the living room. Richard had escaped. The first time she'd been able to find him since he'd abandoned them, and he'd escaped. He'd been at the dance where they'd met, a middle-aged man easily singled out from the teenagers. She'd stalked him slowly, moving a step and then stopping, hardly discernible in the pulsing light. She'd been reaching for his shoulder, her mouth wide, her lips pulled back from her teeth, when he'd turned, stumbled backward, gasping.

"We miss you," she'd said, her voice penetrating through the thumping bass of the music.

His mouth had twisted into a grimace, pulling the rest of his face with it. Then, he'd screamed and Victoria looked down. The skin of her reaching arm was slashed open almost to the bone, the blood dripping lazily, her skin sallow white where it wasn't smeared crimson. Then, she'd looked back at him and his mouth was still open in silence, then he'd disappeared. Victoria stood, frozen for a moment, then clawed at her face when she blinked and found herself back in the apartment's bathroom where it had all started. Or ended.

Victoria's eyes roamed around the living room, narrowed, searching. The little monster was here somewhere. She ground her teeth, the scraping sound making Lucy cover her ears in her hiding spot. There were only so many places the girl could hide. Victoria angrily swatted her hair away from her face. The coffee table had been pulled away from the couch.

Victoria's jaw clenched. One moment, the couch was there, sagging in the middle, the next, it wasn't. Lucy yelped, jumped up, trying to run to her room. But she couldn't get past Victoria, who grabbed one of her arms, pulling Lucy back and seizing the other arm, like they were going to play Monkey Flip. Instead of letting Lucy walk up her body to flip over backward, Victoria stood on the little monster's feet and started pulling. Lucy screamed.

She struggled against her mother, but began to stretch, the pain overwhelming her instinct to escape. Her arms, thin little girl arms to begin with, grew thinner as they elongated. Her legs, too, lengthened, her knees pulling past the cuffs of her pink jeans, her favorites, the ones with Cinderella on the left leg. She cried, mucus clogging her nose so she breathed in choking bursts.

Victoria wondered how far she could pull, picturing the taffy her parents had bought her on Mackinac Island when she was a child, the stretch, the snap and curl of the thread too thin to support itself. She'd been pulling slowly, but with the image of the torn taffy in mind, she yanked up on Lucy's arms and her body distended along with her arms and legs, and Victoria found herself eye to eye with Lucy. Victoria frowned, but wasn't too disappointed. There were still lessons to be learned, and she had plenty of time to teach them now. Her jaw still clenched, she smiled joylessly.

She let go of Lucy, who collapsed down into coils, unable to hold herself up.

"Get up."

Lucy could not.

"Get up now. You're fine."

And she was, her arms, legs and body back to the proportions they should be. But Lucy's elbows and knees still ached and her stomach didn't feel like it was in the right place. The little girl stood, and she dragged the underside of her nose across her forearm, the fine hairs now plastered against her skin. She blinked and a tear slid down her cheek, which she hurriedly wiped away.

"Now," Victoria said. "To your lessons. Start with the bathroom. You made such an awful mess in there."

Lucy rose without a word, trudged past her mother, who followed and then disappeared into her bedroom.

The bathroom was indeed a mess. Water had overflowed the tub, staining the floor a reddish green. The mirror was broken, the glass crunching under her sneakers, the frog statue on its side, staring up at her. More red stains dotted the walls and the tub, drained of water, had a faint crimson ring high up on the plastic.

Lucy started crying, putting a hand over her mouth and moaning through it, afraid that her mother would hear. It wasn't the pain from the stretching. She just always cried when she was in the bathroom.

She stopped crying, hearing someone else crying, laughing. It wasn't her mother's high, thin voice. It was deeper, like her daddy's, but not his.

Then, wavering, as if seen from underwater, she saw the man that she'd talked to before, kneeling in front of the sink. She couldn't tell what he was doing, but he glowed a dark yellow, moving jerkily.

She moved over next to him. Standing up on her tiptoes, she looked into the sink.

It was full of little things, colored grossly green, purple, dark red. Lucy yelped, swatting at one that was bigger than the others, spiky and crawling up the side of the sink. It fell into the swirling water, which washed it down the drain. A red spike poked back out of the drain and she clapped her hand over it. It tickled the palm of her hand, felt sharp as it poked. Then, it was gone and the man had stopped crying, turned off the water.

"What are you doing?" she asked, pulling her hand off of the drain.

The man stood up, looked right at her, through her.

"I said, what are you doing?"

"Oh, it's you," he said, crossing the room to the bathtub, which was clean now. "I was just, uh—washing my hands."

Lucy sat on the edge of the tub to talk to him, reaching down to touch, unfelt, the side of his face, run her fingers through his thin, blonde hair. She tried to take his glasses off, so she could look through them, but couldn't quite grasp them. "Oh. Okay."

The man leaned away from her over the tub. "I thought you'd left for school. Not feeling well?"

Above them, growing unseen from the wall was an ear, surrounded by a few strands of wiry black hair. On the other side of the wall, in her bedroom, Victoria listened to her daughter's conversation, to the man's responses, more fatherly than Richard had ever been, and she smiled.

9

Over the last hour or so, Bob O'Neill's secretary, his daughter Janie, had been sneaking the volume of the radio up a little bit at a time. It slowly dawned on Bob that he wasn't really reading Applewood's monthly bills anymore, but nodding in time with a thumping bass drum beat, humming guitar and vocal harmonies. Heaving a sigh, he hefted his rotund body out of his chair, which creaked, and stuck his head through the open doorway. Twelve years ago, when he'd bought the Applewood Apartments, he'd had the door to the manager's office taken off, welcoming everyone. Now he wished he hadn't.

"Jane?" he said, then repeated himself louder when she failed to turn around. With his voice still raised, he said, "Could you turn that down, please? I can hardly hear myself think."

"Dad," she whined, refusing to raise her voice because that would admit her father was right. "I can barely hear it."

"Jane," he said, sticking to their daily dialogue, "I can hear it in my office and I know that my hearing is worse than yours. So, please turn it down." Then, just to shake things up a little, he added, "And here at the office, you should really call me Mr. O'Neill."

Janie turned the radio down a little. Rolling her eyes, she asked, "Shouldn't you call me Ms. Gunn, then?"

"If I called you anything, it'd be Ms. O'Neill."

"Not anymore," she said. "I'm getting it changed legally. I have the form and everything."

"Just keep it down to a dull roar," he said, back on script.

Bob made it all the way back to his desk and was about to sit down when the radio volume cranked. Hands on the arms of the chair, he reversed direction, pushing himself up and his chair back, which smacked against the wall. He dodged around the desk, nimble in his annoyance. He came out of the office, pushed past his daughter, who squawked in protest when he shut the radio off.

"But it's Aerosmith!" she answered his furious expression. "How could you turn off Aerosmith?"

"Because," he said, that great parental stand by. "I'm sick of needing to tell you over and over again. If you want this job, you need to take it seriously. If not, I can find someone else. There are plenty of people who need a job right now."

This part of their ongoing argument happened about every other week.

"Alright," Janie said, properly chastened for now. "Can I turn it back on if I keep it low?"

Satisfied that he'd done right and that he'd be listened to this time, Bob said, "Well, I suppose so. But if I have to come back out here, that's it."

"Okay."

Bob nodded and went back into the office to finish the bills. Property insurance had gone up this quarter. It was stupid: his premium had jumped after his last claim six years ago, when a falling tree had ripped some shingles off the roof of one of the buildings, and it just kept going up, even though he hadn't had another claim since. The water bill had gone up again too. Not enough to make tenants pay for water, but just enough to make Bob consider charging another quarter to do laundry.

When he finished the bills, he paused, listening carefully, but Janie hadn't turned up the music at all, even a little. Even a barely discernible increase in volume would be enough for him to put off his last chore of the day. He put it off all week, every week but even though Bob was a horrible procrastinator, he would never shirk his duty. Heaving a sigh, he signed into complaints@applewoodapartments.com.

There were only three new emails, which he considered to be a small miracle.

The first one was about number 14 over in building 2, an upstairs one bedroom. There'd been a loud party last weekend, which had kept the occupant of 12, the apartment below 14, up until practically dawn. Bob rolled his eyes. He would have been shocked if someone had pointed out the uncanny resemblance to his daughter in that moment. He checked 14's file, found a phone number and dialed, got a machine, left the standard message.

"Hello, Mr. Shackelford, Bob O'Neill here. Just wanted to let you know that I received a complaint about a party you hosted last weekend. Even though it was the weekend, I'd just ask you to remain courteous to your neighbors in regards to noise level. Feel free to call me back or email me if you have any questions or concerns of your own. Thanks and have a nice day."

The second email was about someone smoking in the corridor of building 3. Also easy enough to deal with. He blind-copied all of the residents on an email, told them that, as the weather got colder, it was perfectly understandable that people didn't want to smoke outside, but if they chose not to smoke in their apartment because of the smell, then they should imagine how it was for their non-smoker neighbors. Signed, sent, and done.

Bob smiled, rubbed his pudgy hands together, but then frowned. This was too easy.

Sure enough, the last email was titled 'Freak in the Laundry Room.' He opened it, his stomach dropping in anticipation. All doors were supposed to stay shut and locked; each resident had keys. Sometimes, though, a door wouldn't close all the way, a homeless person or other kind of drifter would find his way in and end up scaring one of the residents. That didn't seem to be the case this time, though.

Mr. O'Neill,

I'm writing this to you as I sit at the coin-op laundry down Grand River, waiting for my shirts to dry and I'm already 20 minutes late for work. I went to do my laundry this morning, and some guy was in there, running all of the washing machines empty and pouring bleach in all of them. I don't know what the hell his problem is, but now I'm late and my boss hung up on me when I called to tell him what was going on. The guy is white, blonde with glasses, pretty average looking. He said something about the machines being dirty. I don't know if he lives here, if he needs help or what, but if he does live here, I think someone should explain to him that they are washing machines.

I need to stop now. My shirts are done. But I will be calling soon as I can to make sure that this is dealt with because this is bullshit. 33 minutes and counting.

Irina Johnson

That one made up for all of the complaints that he hadn't gotten this week. Usually, people wrote in all caps when they were pissed online. Even though Ms. Johnson hadn't, Bob felt a fire under his ass to do something immediately, especially since she'd emailed him yesterday, promising a follow-up. If he could preempt that with a solution, he could go home and actually enjoy his weekend. Otherwise, he'd fret about it, compulsively check his email and voicemail. He exited his office.

"I haven't even touched the volume knob!" Janie said when she saw him come out.

"No, it's not that," he said, all business. "There haven't been any phone messages today, have there?"

Picking up his seriousness, she replied, "No. I mean, that guy from the tree removal service called while you were at lunch, but I gave you that message." A pause, full of self-doubt. When he didn't reply, she confirmed, "Right?"

"What? Oh, yeah. You did." He pursed his lips, thinking. "If a Ms. Irina Johnson calls, tell her I'm not here. I'll call her back as soon as I take care of something." He started to go back into the office, and then stopped. "But don't tell her that. Just tell her I'm not here."

He went back to his desk and reread the email and thought. After finishing a third read through, he leaned forward, grabbed his stress ball shaped like an alien, sat back and started squeezing. Its eyes and ears bugged out and he couldn't help but smile.

A guy. That could describe three quarters of his tenants. Blonde narrowed it down, but wearing glasses wasn't a big help. He didn't know who wore contacts and who didn't, who might wear glasses when they first got up. Average looking could pretty much describe anyone who lived at Applewood.

...something about the machines being dirty.

And it's so... clean!

Everything clicked into place. Clarence Gottlieb, building 1, apartment 6. Bob remembered the unit tour because he'd almost let slip what had happened. Luckily, Clarence hadn't asked any questions and obviously hadn't done any research, even though it wasn't a big deal. It was just a hard sell to most people, and Bob didn't want to take any chances with the apartment sitting empty for another five months, or even more.

Mulling over the problem for another minute, Bob came to a decision, reached for his phone.

She picked up on third ring, "Hello?"

"Hello, Ms. Johnson, this is Bob O'Neill from Applewood Apartments. How are you today?"

Irritation sharpened her voice. "Better than

yesterday, Bob, but still pretty pissed."

"I understand your annoyance, Ms. Johnson. I just wanted you to know that the problem has been addressed."

"Well, what's going to happen?" While Bob fumbled for an answer, she continued, "I think he at least owes me an apology. You know I was an hour late to work. I count on working all of my hours, you know. So…"

The way she trailed off, insinuating that she should be reimbursed for her poor planning itched under Bob's skin, but his voice was even when he took a chance and lied, "I was told that he already apologized, Ms. Johnson."

"I—what? I mean—"

"Did he apologize to you?"

"I don't know." The silence was heavy with her growing anger. "I guess. I can't really remember. I was pretty pissed, you know."

"I understand, Ms. Johnson."

When he left it at that, she said, "Well, could you, like, tell me which apartment he's in? I wasn't in a good place to accept an apology yesterday, but if I can talk to him, maybe—"

"Out of the question, I'm afraid," Bob said. "We can't give out that kind of information." When she didn't say anything further, he continued, "I assure, the problem has been addressed, and I hope that you will accept my apology, in addition to his."

"I—I… Fine! Good-bye."

Definitely not the way he had hoped it would

go, but still. Given a couple days, he was sure Ms. Johnson would move on, finding something new to get stressed out about.

As for Bob, it was still twelve minutes to six, but close enough as far as he was concerned.

10

This was it. Clarence sat in his car in the parking lot of Warilow's, where Val had told him to meet her and Mike at six o'clock.

"It's got a blue awning," she'd said when she'd called around three. Then, she'd laughed. "Actually, we used to call it Blue Awning, 'cause whenever we'd go there, we'd get so smashed that we couldn't remember how to pronounce the name."

After talking to Lucy, Clarence had spent the afternoon researching bars online. "It won't be too crowded, will it?" he'd asked Val. Then, showing off his new vocabulary, he'd said, "I like my bars pretty chill."

She'd laughed again, which had relaxed him. A little.

"Yeah, it's pretty chill. I mean, there's karaoke starting at nine, but Mike and I usually bug out before that. Too many people who think they can sing, but American Idols they ain't." When Clarence couldn't think of what to say, she misinterpreted his silence. "Unless you like, want to stick around. Do you sing?"

He'd shuddered at the idea, but managed to say, "Only in the shower."

She'd laughed obligingly, given him the address and told him that they'd be there for happy hour around six. He'd told her he'd see them there, then had a panic attack and washed his hands for ten minutes.

Clarence got out of his car, cleaned it, then stood, feet frozen in place, surveying the bar. It had a small parking lot, was a small building with two entrances, one on the front under its blue awning, which was actually more of a purplish color, and one on the side. Val hadn't told him which entrance to go to.

To calm himself, he touched the outside of his pockets, checking his supplies. He had a fresh packet of Lysol wipes in his right pocket, a package of Kleenex in the left, along with a brand new bottle of hand sanitizer. In his back pocket, he had a pair of plastic gloves in case of an emergency. Even so, he was sweating lightly.

Clarence decided to go in the back door, was afraid that people would turn around and stare at him if he went in the front. Maybe if he could slip in, no one would notice.

The smell hit him when he opened the door and he almost turned right around and left. There was the high, sharp smell of fried food, and the lower odors of yeast and sweat. Breathing shallowly so he didn't gag, Clarence went inside.

The bar looked exactly like the photos of it online. The main room had a long bar on one side, tables, no booths, and a tiled empty area in the middle. In the pictures, couples had been dancing in this area. They'd also shown a back room, which he couldn't see from where he stood.

The pictures had shown a crowded bar, that this was a popular place to see and be seen by the cool people, but at six o' clock on a Friday, it was pretty chill, which made Clarence relax slightly. And no one was staring at him. His heart hammered a little softer and he didn't press his palms against his thighs quite so hard.

Mike sat facing the front door, Val faced the side door. She drummed her fingers against the table in a staccato rhythm and he rolled his beer glass between his hands, both excited to get the game underway.

Val straightened in her chair and waved. Mike turned around, saw Clarence and waved too. Clarence didn't wave or nod, just started walking toward them, like he was some kind zombie. The happiest zombie not-alive.

"Remember," Val said from behind Mike, "legit."

"Yeah, yeah."

On the drive over, they'd debated what constituted a legit stolen five. It needed to be a full, palm to palm slap. Grazing fingers didn't count. Mutual fives didn't count. And when one of them went to the bathroom, it was an automatic time out.

"Or else, our kidneys will explode," Val had joked.

Clarence saw Val waving at him from a table near the front door, Mike turning around and waving too. Blushing and grinning, he crossed the room. Luckily the bar had a nice, wide aisle to walk down. He stood beside the table for an awkward minute, looking at Mike and Val, both of them smiling, happy to see him, and Clarence thought he could die happy right now.

After about a minute of him standing there, staring at them, Val's smile started to falter. "Hey, uh—Clarence. Why don't you take a load off? Stay awhile?"

"Okay," he said, bobbing his head and pushing his glasses up on his nose, which immediately slid back down. He pulled the chair out with two fingers, sat on as little of the seat as possible, on the very edge, his back ramrod straight and his hands on his thighs. Then, he continued staring at them.

"How you doing?" Mike asked.

"I'm fairly well, thank you. How are you?"

"I'm okay."

"Yeah, okay," Val chimed in.

"So, uh—what'd you get up to today?" Mike asked him, sipping his beer.

"You know, the usual."

"No, we don't know," Val said, taking a drink of her Jim and coke and leaning back. "What's a day in the life of Clarence… What's your last name, dude?"

"Gottlieb," he replied. "Well, I'm not sure what time I got up today. I had a nightmare—"

"Really?" Val interrupted. She didn't dream, at least that she remembered. "What was the nightmare about?"

"I was, uh, reading this Poe story, The Masque of Red Death." Clarence paused, unsure how much to tell them. "I just had a dream about it."

"Poe who? The musician?" Mike asked.

"Who?"

"What?"

"You know," Mike said. "That one hot chick."

"Oh," Val said. "You think anyone with more than a B-cup is hot."

"No I don't!"

"What? No," Clarence said. "Edgar Poe was an author in the 19th century—"

"Oh," Mike said. "Yeah, I know him." Then, his voice brightened. "They did that poem on The Simpsons, didn't they? I about laughed my balls off!"

"Yeah," Clarence said, nodding and smiling. "I saw that one too."

They kept talking, Clarence mostly, Mike and Val asking questions, hoping that Clarence would relax and take his hands off of his thighs to give them a chance. Then, Val realized why he was sitting so straight and so still.

"Hey!" she exclaimed, making both of the men jump. "You don't have a drink!"

"Oh. Yeah," Clarence said, looking around. "I guess the waiter's busy. I didn't think it was that crowded in here."

He was right. People came in, other people left and more came in to replace them, but the overall size of the crowd didn't change. Clarence craned his neck around to look for someone he could wave over. Now that Val had said something, his mouth was arid from all the talking. Even so, he was in heaven. He had friends! When he looked back at them, Val was looking at him, one eyebrow cocked.

"Sorry, kiddo. No waitress til the karaoke crowd gets here." She stood up. "What're you drinking? First round's on me." She caught Mike's eye and mouthed the word, "Timeout."

He nodded, then said, "Jim and coke."

"Oh I get it," Val said, teasing. "Not such a cheap ass when it ain't your money, huh?"

Mike stuck his tongue out.

"What about you, Clarence?"

"Water's fine. Thank you."

Val's jaw dropped. "No, seriously. What do you want? It's okay, I'm buying."

"Oh." Clarence puffed his cheeks out, then whistled. "Milk? Skim, if they have it."

Val sat back down and Mike leaned forward. They said, only slightly not in unison, "You don't drink?" "Don't you drink?"

"I, uh—I don't know." He started blushing, his fingers gripping the cleaning supplies in his pockets. Then, he sat up a little straighter, smiling slightly. "I just don't, you know, want to drink and drive."

Mike nodded, begrudging approval mixed with guilt. "Yeah. I can respect that."

"Totally," Val agreed. "Milk it is. Hey Mike, could you give me a hand with the drinks?" When he looked at her blankly, she said, "One, two, three and—" She held up her hands and shook them a little.

"Yeah, alright."

"Want me to help?" Clarence asked, scooting his chair back from the table.

"No, we got it. You just—" she looked him up and down, his militant posture, hands neatly on his lap, all three buttons of his polo buttoned, the creases in his slacks worn smooth on his thighs, sharp as a razor down the rest of his leg. "You just relax."

Val and Mike went up to the bar and ordered the drinks. Mike looked at his watch. They'd been here for about an hour.

"And he hasn't moved a muscle," Mike said.

"What?"

"Clarence. Other than talk, he hasn't moved a friggin' inch since he got here!"

"I know!" She looked over at Clarence, who sat facing forward, not watching them. "He's so fucking weird! And he's not gonna drink. What're we gonna do?"

"I'll tell you what we're gonna do," Mike said, then turned away, beckoning the bartender over. He took a moment to try to peek down her halter top, then said, "Hey, yeah, can you drop a little Bailey's in that milk?"

"That's below the belt, man."

"Well, what do you wanna do?" Mike demanded. The bartender stood there, not saying anything.

Val thought for a minute, then turned to the bartender. "Milk, for now." Then, looking back at Mike, she said, "Just follow my lead."

Val paid for the drinks and they took them back to the table.

While Mike and Val were waiting for the

drinks up at the bar, Clarence thought about leaving. Maybe this hadn't been such a good idea after all. When he'd told them about his nightmare, Val had leaned in, looked like she wanted to pat him on the shoulder or on the leg. Mike made him uncomfortable too, the way that he kept looking at Clarence's hands, as if he knew that Clarence was diseased and was keeping a wary eye on him.

Clarence weighed the pros and cons, taking a peek over his shoulder. They were talking with the bartender. Val looked mad. He took the opportunity to sanitize his hands. In the end, he decided that Lucy was right: he needed friends; and, this really wasn't any different than working with them everyday.

Besides, if he was infecting them, the damage had already been done.

His breath shortened and he took another peek over his shoulder. Val was paying for the drinks. Clarence took out the wipes packet, got one out and cleaned the table, stuffing it into his pocket and re-sanitizing his hands. He hunched his shoulders when he heard them coming.

Val set Clarence's milk in front of him on a table that shone with moisture, smelled like evergreen. She cocked an eyebrow at Clarence, who blushed the brightest shade of red she'd ever seen. Mike didn't look amused, but Val couldn't help but smile.

"Thanks Clarence," she said, nonchalantly. "Christ knows the last time they cleaned this table."

By degrees, Clarence's shoulders settled, his blush ebbed and he smiled too, a grin that spread from one side of his face to the other, pushing his glasses up on his cheeks. He sipped his milk, not taking his eyes off of Val, who took a big gulp of her new Jim and coke, not noticing the way that Clarence was looking at her.

Mike saw, however, and he didn't like it. He watched Clarence's hand carefully as he set the glass back on the table then placed it back on his thigh. The game needed to end, and soon.

"You know, Clarence," Val began, "if you wanted to drink, I could give you a ride home. I mean, Mike drove me, so he could just follow us. I could drive your car and—"

The look on Clarence's face made her choke on her words. His smile disappeared and his eyes widened. His mouth curled into a half-snarl, half-sneer and he leaned forward. What scared Mike was that the guy seemed to stop breathing.

"Excuse me, I need to go to the bathroom," he managed to gasp, lurching up from the table and grabbing his glass of milk so that he wouldn't leave his germs at the table.

He was in the bathroom already before he realized he hadn't cleaned the door where he'd pushed it open. The fresh scent of the Lysol wipes contrasted to the urine smell, comforting him, and he snuck the door open a little ways and reached out to surreptitiously wipe it clean.

"Did you see that?" Mike asked, slapping his glass down onto the table.

"What?"

"He reached out to clean the door. Okay, okay—this is just too fucking weird. The guy's a—"

"Are you saying you forfeit?" Val asked, leaning over the table.

"No, I—god damn it Val, the guy's a complete nutjob. You saying he doesn't creep you the hell out?"

Clarence did, but she said, "Nope."

Mike sputtered, but couldn't think of anything to say without telling her about the way that Clarence had looked at her, that he was jealous. Val would never let him live it down. So he shut his mouth and kept rolling his glass between his hands.

In the bathroom, Clarence paced, trying to think of how to handle this. He needed to leave, right now. He thought he'd been handling it well, but the idea of Val driving him home in his filthy car was too much. They'd know where he lived, would probably want to come in, even to go to the bathroom. He had his new hands-free soap dispensers, but by now, a single germ that had managed to survive the cleaning today had probably multiplied into a contagion engine, covering everything and it was just too much. He needed to go home and clean. Now.

Clarence had been taking nervous sips of his milk as he paced and thought. Now, he drank the last of it, then went to the sink and washed it with hand sanitizer. Eventually, the sound of running water and the fresh, clean smell soothed his galloping heart.

He put on the clear plastic gloves from his pocket. They conformed to his hands and, except for some wrinkling at the fingertips, practically disappeared.

He took his washed glass and set it on the bar, thanking the bartender who looked at him, at the glass, then back at him. Then, he walked over to Mike and Val, who sat up at his approach. Mike's eyes narrowed as Clarence stood at the table, his hands clasped behind his back.

"I'm sorry, but I'm not feeling very well. I think I'm going to go home and clean." He snapped his mouth shut, wishing he could take the words back, that they wouldn't think he was a freak, like that woman from the laundry room.

Mike got Val's attention and nodded toward Clarence as if to say, see? See?

Val ignored him, started to reach out to pat Clarence on the arm, but stopped when he jerked away from her. "Oh you poor baby. Sure you're not just hungry or something? It's getting about that time."

Food was the last thing on Clarence's mind right now. "No. I'm not hungry. Just need to lie down, I think. I'll see you guys."

Clarence walked away before they could offer him high-fives. With his back to them, he was able to sanitize his gloved hands without them seeing before touching the door handle and exiting the bar. He held it together the entire drive home and into his apartment. There, greeted by the hum of his air purifiers, the still lingering clean scent masking the deathly stench of his germs he knew must be there, waiting, he fell to his knees and wept.

Saturday

11

Clarence sat at the bar table in his dining room, reclining in the hard-back chair, at ease. Val sat kitty-corner to him and Mike sat across from him, on the edge of his seat. Mike had his hands clasped together on the table, around a glass of water. On the table in front of Clarence sat a tall frosty mug of beer, condensation trickling down the side, the foamy head pristine. He smirked as he lifted the mug, downed the beer in one long gulp, Val looking at him, wanting him. Clarence didn't have to see it to know it was true. The same went for the look of envy on Mike's face.

Clarence slammed the mug down, which made Mike jump. He took a small sip of water, and Clarence threw his head back and laughed at him.

"Why did you come to a bar if you didn't want to drink?" Clarence demanded.

"I—I di—idn't want to dri—ink and d—drive."

Val sighed.

Clarence's smirk widened as he downed the new mug of beer that appeared before him. "Yeah," he conceded. "I guess I can respect that."

"If you want to drink," Val said, leaning forward but not able to bring herself to touch Mike, "I can drive you home. Clarence drove me. I mean, I'd rather just go home with him than have to take care of you, but we understand if you want to take a break from being a weirdo."

Mike hunkered down into his seat and Clarence felt himself grow that much taller. He slammed another beer and belched, like real men do. Val sighed again, caressed his arm and he didn't jerk away from her. Instead, he pulled her to him, tipping back in the chair which reclined as she straddled him. Mike watched them, tears welling up. Clarence wanted him to watch as much as he wanted Val to run her hands up and down his chest, unbutton his shirt, lean down and kiss him…

Val was unbuckling his belt while Mike groaned when a quiet voice asked, "What are you doing?"

Clarence tipped forward in his chair, Val no longer on top of him or even in the room. Mike had vanished as well. He sat at his dining table, dark-wood Ikea, four matching chairs with cream-colored seat cushions.

She sat on her feet, her hands on her knees, on the floor in front of an older television, which wasn't his. The whole living room wasn't his: the striped couch, its cushions lumpy and uncomfortable looking; the bookshelf full of Disney DVDs and Danielle Steele; the glass coffee table with a half-empty cup of juice on it.

The girl's jet hair was wet, plastered flat against her head like she'd just gotten out of the bath and she was dressed in pink jeans and a white top. Her eyes were small for her face, which made her look suspicious of him. There was something familiar in the way she held her body, her hands on her thighs, shoulders hunched, as if in anticipation of something bad.

"I was, uh—just pretending, I guess," he replied. "What are you doing in my apartment?"

The girl tipped her head to the side, puzzled by this when the idea of an adult pretending didn't seem to bother her a bit. "Clarence?"

Clarence blinked. "How do you know my name?"

The girl squealed and leapt to her feet, running across the room. Clarence knew he should be worried about her clear intention to hug him, but caught her instead. Something about her made such things seem trivial. Replaying her few words in his mind, he held her at arm's length.

"Lucy?" Once he subtracted the tinny reverberation, there was no mistaking her voice.

She returned his stare. "You don't look like a prince."

"What?"

"You know," she said, spinning away from him, her hands clasped together. "The brave prince comes to stand up to the wicked queen and rescue the fair princess and the two of them live happily ever after." Lucy stood next to the coffee table, caressing a statue of a frog. Turning shy, she cocked one shoulder like an eyebrow, peering coyly at him.

"Certainly, m'lady," Clarence said, joining in the game, smiling. He stood, then bowed, sweeping his cape away from his body with one hand, touching his heart with the other. "Long and longer have I travelled to find you. And now that I have, let me take you away from the troubles that beset you."

Lucy giggled, now dressed in a flowing dress, with a tall, pointed cap with a veil. She held her hand out to Clarence, who swept across the stone floor, dodging the corner of the couch. He clasped her hands in his. She gazed up at him, then snapped her head around toward the hall, the bedrooms, when she heard a thump.

Clarence looked, the stone floor blending into the carpet that led to the back of the apartment. The bedroom door was closed, in shadow from the afternoon sun. There was nothing sinister about it; it was just a door. All the same, Clarence felt his stomach drop, like when his father used to yell at him and he knew he was in big trouble. Now, like then, he wanted to run, hide and pretend that he didn't exist.

Lucy pulled on his hands, getting his attention. "The queen awakens! We must flee!" She started to dash away, but Clarence's grip had tightened when his stomach dropped and she was pulled back. "Quick! The couch didn't work, but we both can't fit behind the movie shelf. You hide in the closet. Over there!"

Something was coming. On the other side of the door, some malicious presence had awakened and was turning its attention to them. Clarence looked at the bookshelf. He didn't see how she could fit behind it at all. Also, he doubted that they could hide from whatever was coming. It would seek them out, an ear for their breathing, a nose for their fear.

"No," he said, the faint click of the bedroom's knob and his own heartbeat loud in his ears. "Come on!" Clarence held her protesting hands tighter, pulled her toward the door.

"No! The fog—"

Clarence opened the door on the afternoon sun. They ran out onto the grass of an urban field, a playground a short distance away. The door slammed shut behind them and vanished, leaving them with a stalking feeling of frustration that quickly burned away in the afternoon sun.

Clarence wore shorts and a tie-dye t-shirt, an explosion of red, yellow and orange, that he remembered well from this summer, when he'd been ten. On his feet, he wore sneakers dirty with the summer days. He hadn't worn glasses back then, but still felt their subtle weight on his nose.

Lucy was in her jeans and t-shirt again, her eyes sparkling with tears. She looked up at Clarence, her eyes widened, no longer suspicious. "Oh, Clarence! Are we going to play?"

In answer, Clarence grinned, feeling a forgotten thrill of adventure. Before he could answer, a boy blew between them, racing toward the playground.

"Last one there's a shithead!"

"Hey, Mickey, wait up!" Clarence called out of long-forgotten habit, running after him.

Instead of running to the slide or monkey bars

or swings, Mickey ran to the crabapple trees that stood on the border of the parking lot. He leapt, grabbing onto a branch, his feet scrabbling against the trunk. He swung up and sat on a branch, picked the nearest crabapple and aimed. Clarence, running full speed, didn't see it coming, just skidded to a stop and put a hand to his forehead.

"Ow! What the hell—"

"Got you!" Mickey called, throwing another crabapple, missing on purpose to laugh at Clarence when he ducked wildly.

"Ha ha! You missed!"

Clarence covered his head and ran for the nearest tree. He scrambled up into the tree, picking some ammunition and chucking it at Mickey. Most of the crabapples ricocheted off the trees' branches and fell, but one hit Mickey in the butt as he moved to a different branch. He swore and Clarence grinned, tasting sweet revenge.

"Clarence," Lucy called from the ground under his tree.

She jumped to grab the lowest branch, but couldn't quite reach. Clarence got down, landing heavily next to her. He put his hands on her waist and boosted her up into the tree. The rough bark bit into her tender hands deliciously, and she winced with a huge smile on her face when she turned back to look at Clarence. He nodded and waved at her to move further up so he could climb back up.

When they were sitting side by side, Lucy reached and plucked an apple from its stem. She tossed it and caught it, squinting one eye and taking aim through the branches. She threw the crabapple so hard she almost fell, but Clarence caught her.

"Son of a bitch!" Mickey cried when the apple pegged him on the ass again.

Clarence and Lucy laughed, giving each other a high five. The satisfying slap stung his palm and rustled the leaves on the trees. He reached into his pocket and pulled out a package of Sour Patch Kids, his favorite. That summer, he always had a bag with him, even though his mother said that they'd rot his teeth. And he always shared. Except for the yellow ones. Those were his most favorite.

He held the open bag out to Lucy, who reached in. "I call dibs on the yellow ones."

Lucy nodded and separated out two yellow ones, giving them back to him. They sat, eating candy, laughing when crabapples made it through the leaves only to be easily dodged, or miss completely.

"Dude," Clarence taunted, watching one sail by. "That's just sad."

"Piss off," Mickey called. "Can I have some Kids?"

"Sure," Clarence said.

"No!" Lucy said. "The black knight shall not share our bounty."

"As you wish m'lady."

"What is she, your girlfriend?"

It was the question that every boy had to deal with if he was caught even smiling at a girl, let alone talking to her. Clarence felt the familiar embarrassment.

"No! She's just a friend!"

"Lucy and Clarence, sitting in a tree," Mickey sang. "K-I-S-S—"

"Shut up!" Clarence yelled, knowing that the more he denied it, the more Mickey would make fun of him, but still unable to help himself.

"So, why was she in your apartment?" Mickey asked.

Clarence opened his mouth to answer, then shut it slowly. He turned to Lucy, who sat on the branch beside him, plucking leaves from a twig and tearing them to shreds.

"Why were you in his apartment?" Mickey asked her.

Lucy looked at Clarence. "I don't know. I was watching SpongeBob when I heard you playing pretend behind me."

"What was behind the door?" Mickey asked, his voice lower.

"The queen," she answered. "She spends a lot of time in her room when she's not out looking for the king." She let her chin drop to her chest, her black hair falling forward to hide her face. "Or punishing me."

She took a shaking breath, whooshed it out. "She heard us talking. You know, the last time, when you said I should ask her to let me go outside and play." Lucy turned to face him, her eyes swimming. "She was real mad."

Gray fog blew across everything, leeching the green from the leaves, the blue from the sky. Clarence and Lucy floated in the air for a moment before the fog pulled back and formed into walls, covered with posters. The ceiling was painted an eggshell white and a fan turned lazily. Clarence whuffed softly, settling into the bed that coalesced beneath him. Lucy stood in the corner, unsure of what had happened, shy again.

Clarence's mother bustled around the room, her forehead beaded with sweat, despite the fan moving the air. She frowned, putting toys and books back on the shelves. He watched her from his place under the covers, loving everything about her.

"Are you mad at me?" Clarence asked.

"No," she answered, too quickly. "I'm just—frustrated. You're supposed to be outside having fun. Not cooped up in here with a fever, worrying your father and me."

"I'm sorry," Clarence said, snuggling down into the covers when she pulled them up to his chin. "I promise I'll try to go the rest of the summer without getting sick."

His mother laughed, tucking a sweaty curl of her short hair behind her ear. Immediately, it fell free and Clarence was so struck by the familiarity of this that he squeezed his eyes shut, unable to look at her without crying. This is when it had happened, he knew now, when it had started. And it was all his fault.

"Look at this room!" His mom spread her arms and swung them around. Clarence obeyed and looked around. It was just his room, he'd thought then. "I swear there's dust in here left over from when the place was built!" She picked up his stuffed dog, fresh from the wash and razzed him with it, Clarence laughing.

In the corner, Lucy yearned to be Clarence in this moment. She was also scared, feeling something was wrong. Clarence laughed, but his cheeks were wet with tears. Only his mother still smiled, surrounded by dim, dark purple light.

"It's no wonder you get sick," Clarence's mother said after she tucked Dog under the covers. Crossing the room, she stopped by the open door, said, "You know, if you only cleaned up after yourself once in awhile, you might not get sick so often."

She coughed then, really only clearing her throat. But Clarence knew better.

His mother shut the door softly behind her, but the click of the latch screamed in the long, monotone wail of a heart monitor, drowning out Clarence's voice as he screamed, his face turning red, then purple as his stomach muscles clenched, lifting him off the bed.

Lucy slapped her hands over her ears, screaming too. Falling to her knees, she squeezed her eyes shut and ducked her head as the windows shattered, the walls exploded and the floor collapsed beneath her. Clarence vanished, and the splintered remains of the room dissolved into gray fog, which swirled around the little girl.

Although she didn't feel like she was falling, she felt a drifting weightlessness, until her feet touched a firmer nothing in the gray void. Lucy stood, turning this way and that, unsure where to go, since everything looked the same.

Lucy walked, following the path of her instinct. Shadows loomed in the mist, of a tree, bent and misshapen, a bed, low and creeping. She raced toward these visions, scared, but still eager to find something of substance in the gray. But the shadows faded, and she let them come when she thought of them, then fade, unable to hold onto anything.

Her feet aching inside her sneakers, she saw another shadow and plodded toward it without any real hope of reaching it. It solidified as she got closer, and the first butterfly of hope fluttered in her stomach. It was impossible to keep from running toward the door standing freely in the fog.

Lucy stood in front of it, circled it. It looked familiar, a white painted door with four panels evenly spaced and brass hardware, the knob worn dull from many hands. She grasped the knob and turned it, pushing the door open and feeling her stomach drop.

Her mother stood on the other side, fists on her hips. She seized Lucy and dragged her into the apartment.

"Where have you been? How dare you scare mother like that."

12

Mr. Caruthers stopped climbing, halfway between the basement and the first floor of the Haimes Building. His head swam and he leaned against the bare cinderblock wall. His knees still shook, so he sat on the stairs, stretching his left arm out away from his body and feeling the cold sweat bead on his forehead.

He knew he was out of shape. A man can't not see his feet and think he's fit and fine. But he at least thought that he was a healthy out of shape. He climbed six flights of stairs to the top of the building and back down to the basement at least once a day and yeah, he was a little out of breath by the time he got to the top floor where the executive offices were, but he thought that was perfectly normal.

It had been three years since he'd last seen his doctor. Part of it was the news about his high cholesterol, and the other part was that the building owner cut him back to technically-part-time, which meant that he no longer qualified for health insurance. He hadn't been able to afford the cholesterol medication anymore and wasn't willing to shell out three hundred bucks a year just to be told bad news. He'd done what he could, started packing a salad for lunch instead of going out for fast food and climbing the stairs to the top of the building and back, even on the days when he didn't really need to. He'd lost ten pounds and felt a little better and thought that that was enough.

Now, though, Mr. Caruthers sat on the cold concrete steps halfway between the basement and the first floor, sweating ice cubes while black bugs crawled across his vision and his left arm tingled and if he dropped dead of a heart attack right here, no one would ever know until he started to smell.

The thought of which was not helping to slow his racing heart at all.

After a few minutes, which felt longer, his heart steadied into its regular rhythm and if it seemed different to him, felt different, he was sure that it was just his imagination playing tricks on him.

When he was sure that he wouldn't pass out, Mr. Caruthers stood up and walked back down the half-flight of stairs to the basement. Going to his office, he thumbed through the contact list on his Blackberry, found his doctor's number and dialed on his office phone. If the building owner wouldn't pay for him to go to the doctor, he'd at least pay for the phone call. The ringing in his ear sounded far away.

A sweet-voiced receptionist picked up. "Dr. Schmidt's office, how may I help you?"

Mr. Caruthers cleared his throat. "This is James Caruthers. I'm a patient of Dr. Schmidt's but I—" he blushed, stammered, furious because he was acting like a schoolboy caught making faces at the teacher's back. "I'd like to make an appointment for a physical." His heart thumped, paused, then hammered twice, thump-

thump, to make up for lost time. "Next appointment you have."

"Oh," she said, trying to think of a way to couch the bad news. "Dr. Schmidt is out of town next week, and booked until mid-December. But his associate, Dr. Carlisle, is available in two weeks, the Tuesday after Thanksgiving."

Mr. Caruthers made an unhappy noise in his throat. "Yeah, okay. If you have any cancellations before that…"

"I'll be sure to call and let you know." She paused, the moment pregnant with concern. "Mr. Caruthers, if this is an emergency, you shouldn't wait two weeks and hope for a cancellation."

"No, no," he said. "Not an emergency. It's just time to get serious about stuff."

"I understand," she said. "I have you down for the twenty-ninth at two. Okay?"

"Sounds good," he said, forcing optimism into his voice. "Thanks."

Mr. Caruthers hung up and rested his hand on his stomach, stroking, almost lovingly. It was time to get serious about some stuff and he figured that he'd be eating his last ice cream sundae tonight. There was only a little ice cream left anyway and it was silly to let it go to waste. He was going to have lots of chocolate syrup left. That was okay though. He could make chocolate milk. Skim, of course. After all, it was time to get serious.

Heaving a sigh, he pushed himself up and out of his desk chair, which groaned under his weight, his eyes on his feet as he started shuffling toward the door. Mr. Caruthers saw Clarence lurking in the doorway when he got close enough to him that he took a giant step back, the motion catching Mr. Caruthers eye.

He jumped back too, gasping when his heart did what felt like a loop-the-loop in his chest. "Clarence, Jesus! What the hell—you trying to give a heart attack?"

Clarence stood there, his shoulders hunched up to his ears, his head ducked down in that way he had, looking like a little boy who'd gotten caught raiding the cookie jar. He held his hands against his thighs. Clarence's eyes on his shoes, Mr. Caruthers watched his glasses slide down from the bridge of his nose to nearly the tip. Clarence reached up and pushed them back up his nose, brushing hair off his forehead in the same gesture.

"No, sir," he said. "I'm sorry, sir."

Mr. Caruthers couldn't put his finger on it, but there was something about him that looked so brittle, like he was ready to snap in half. All it would take was one push in the wrong direction.

Irritated at being startled and unnerved, Mr. Caruthers covered it in his usual way. "What do you want, Clarence?"

Clarence shuffled his feet. "I'd like to not work with Val and Mike anymore."

"Why?"

"I, uh—they think…" he trailed off, taking a step back, almost as if he had changed his mind about what he wanted to say.

Mr. Caruthers didn't prompt him. He wasn't this guy's fucking shrink.

"They think I'm a freak," Clarence finally finished, barely heard. He took a step forward and repeated, louder, "They think I'm a freak."

Mr. Caruthers slipped into manager-mode and sat in his creaky chair, gesturing for Clarence to also sit. "Do you feel you are being harassed?"

Clarence sat, back straight, hands on his knees. "I—I don't know. How do you know you're being harassed?"

"Tease you about something even after you asked them to stop?"

"No," he replied, blushing and looking at his hands in his lap. "They're actually very nice."

Mr. Caruthers paused, pursed his lips. "Did they call you a freak? Or maybe you overheard them?"

Clarence shook his head slowly.

Now, Mr. Caruthers couldn't help grimacing and rolling his eyes. "Then why do you think they think you're a freak?"

Mr. Caruthers snapped his mouth shut. He started to turn red, his left arm tingling. He didn't know how Clarence had manipulated him, but the questions, standard procedure for an initial investigation of harassment had somehow been turned into a therapy session. He might as well hold out a box of Kleenex and ask Clarence about his relationship with his mother.

Before Clarence could answer, Mr. Caruthers stood, went to the door and opened it. Clarence's mouth hung open like he was about to answer the question.

Mr. Caruthers gestured for Clarence to leave. "You and the wonder twins have a building to clean. Next time you want to waste my time, at least bring me a sandwich or something."

Clarence stood up slowly, his face bright red, making his light blond hair look almost white. He thought he'd be able to talk to Mr. Caruthers about Mike and Val. Maybe even Lucy. Clarence's father had been brusque and dismissive as well, like the one time he'd tried to confess his role in his mother's death to him.

It had been shortly after her funeral and Clarence had been only half-aware of the world for a few days. He'd gotten up one morning—it must've been a Saturday because he didn't think he'd been in a rush to get ready for school—and had gone to the bathroom. After he was done, he'd started to leave, the door open, another day of lackadaisical nothing ahead of him, but he'd paused. He hadn't washed his hands.

Clarence had snatched his hand away from the bathroom doorknob as if it had burned him and stood, staring. He hadn't washed his hands, had gotten his germs all over the doorknob. There was only one bathroom in the house, so sooner or later, his father would come in here and shut the door behind him. Just as his mother must've done a hundred times.

It was irrelevant that he hadn't washed his hands after using the toilet since he was being potty-trained. It was irrelevant that his father had touched the same doorknobs that his mother had, picking up the same germs, and hadn't gotten sick. It was just a matter of time.

Clarence tore open the cabinet doors under the sink, rifling through the bottles, the fact that he had no idea what any of the cleansers were exacerbating his rising panic. He finally settled on the Lysol Multi-Surface and sprayed down the doorknob, wiping it dry with some paper towel. That didn't seem sufficient though, so he cleaned that whole side of the door. Then, the other side, since he was pretty sure he'd touched it coming into the bathroom. Then, the toilet and the sink. But he still hadn't washed his hands, so he did that and cleaned the sink again. Finally, he took all the bottles that he'd touched out of the cabinet and wiped them, one by one.

He'd filled the trash can in the bathroom with wadded paper towels full of his germs. He couldn't leave them there. The germs would multiply, spread, cover the bathroom again and wait. Eager, hungry.

Clarence had taken the can downstairs to empty it in the kitchen trash, then the bigger bag, still half-empty, outside to the can in the garage to wait until trash day.

Coming back in, his father had stopped him and asked, "Was that the trash? Trash day's not 'til Monday."

"I know," Clarence had said, blushing then as he blushed now under Mr. Caruthers's glare.

"Was the bag even full?" his father had asked.

"No, sir."

"What the—" his father had sputtered, his weekend stubble quivering with his irritation. "What the hell is wrong with you?"

Clarence had taken the rare opportunity, even if his father was concerned only out of exasperation. But it was hard to distill the nebulous feeling he had into words. Finally, he said, "I don't want you to die like Mom."

His father had taken off his glasses, so much like the one's Clarence would eventually wear, and pinched the bridge of his nose, squeezing his eyes shut. Clarence had held his breath and rocked forward to stand on the balls of his feet, desperately wanting his father to say that it hadn't been his fault.

"Don't talk to me about her," his father had said, placing his glasses back on his face, tucking the newspaper under his arm and pushing past his eleven-year-old son. Over his shoulder he'd said, "And next time, wait 'til the bag's full. Garbage bags are expensive."

Clarence was close to the door, but Mr. Caruthers wasn't moving. Clarence twisted his body sideways, his shoulders dipped, his hands gripping his thighs so they wouldn't accidentally touch him. Mr. Caruthers folded his arms and rested them on his stomach, his mouth pulling down. The sudden movement made Clarence bump into the doorframe as he stumbled past.

Out of habit, he stopped, pulled a Lysol Wipe from the pouch on his belt and turned to clean where he'd touched.

"What the hell're you doing?" Mr. Caruthers demanded.

"I'm sorry, I—"

"I told you to get to work." He unfolded his arms and held them at his sides, his hands clenched into fists.

"I will. I just have to—"

"No!" Mr. Caruthers shouted, practically into Clarence's face. "Now!"

Clarence stepped back, wincing, tears prickling at the corners of his eyes. "Please sir."

"Now!"

Then, Clarence felt something. His stomach dropped at the thought and he immediately pushed it aside, but then the memory of it wouldn't leave him. He considered just walking away and letting his germs stay on the doorframe, multiply and spread, covering Mr. Caruthers' office, infecting him. He thought about his boss in the hospital, a respirator jammed down his throat, get-well-flowers not allowed in the room because of the pollen, the nurses telling him how nice they looked down at the nurses' station.

Clarence shook his head. No one deserved that. He consciously relaxed his hand which clenched the wipe, squeezing sharp-smelling cleaning solution from it.

Mr. Caruthers didn't relax his glare until Clarence had turned and walked to the elevator. Then, he let out a breath, rubbing his left arm, which ached and tingled.

The air in the basement smelled old and moldy.

He would take it as slow as he needed to, but he needed to get out of here for some fresh air. Usually, he had no problem sitting in his office if he kept the door open because if he started feeling uncomfortable, he could go out into the larger basement. But tonight, he felt the weight of the Haimes Building pushing down on him, wanting to crush him.

Foolish. Still, some fresh air would do him some good.

The stairwell door slammed shut behind him, reverberating off the bare, concrete walls. Once the last echoes had faded, the elevator dinged and the door slid open. Clarence poked his head out and looked around. Not seeing Mr. Caruthers, he hurried over to his boss' office, cleaned the doorframe then scurried back to the elevator.

Clarence pushed the button for the top floor, then wiped it clean. Feeling guilty before he was even aware that he was angry at Mr. Caruthers, Clarence blushed. Another flash of his boss held prisoner in a hospital bed materialized in his mind's eye before Clarence could push it down.

Mike and Val were on the sixth floor, already cleaning. They'd been waiting for Clarence when he'd punched his timecard in the basement. Val had smiled at him but Mike had looked angry, which made Clarence nervous. She had suggested starting on the top floor, and Clarence had nodded. Then, he'd said he'd be right up after he had a word with Mr. Caruthers. Val's expression had changed to concern, but Mike walked away without a word. Val followed him, looking over her shoulder at Clarence.

He wished that he could have talked with Lucy. When he'd snapped awake at what time, he didn't know, he'd gone into the bathroom and called as loudly as he dared, his face nearly touching the bathtub drain. He'd expected her to be awake too, though he didn't know why. Didn't even know why he expected her to know why he had dreamed about her, why it had seemed so real.

Then, as the dream faded as the sun came up and he cleaned his apartment, he'd started thinking about being out with Mike and Val the previous night. His confusion and panic from last night echoed and he realized that he'd need to work with them today. Mr. Caruthers had been almost complimentary when they'd left Thursday night, Mike and Val assuring him that they had been able to clean the whole building, top to bottom.

He'd gone back into the bathroom, calling a little louder than before. But still, there was no answer.

The elevator door opened onto the sixth floor, better carpeting for the executives, more paintings on the walls. Even a little lobby area with four chairs around a coffee table, fichus trees softening each corner. Val sat in one of the chairs while Mike stood, his hands raised and his mouth hanging open like he'd been in the middle of speaking. They both turned their heads when the elevator opened, Val smirking, Mike shutting his mouth and frowning.

"We're done," Mike had said a few minutes before Clarence's arrival.

Val smiled. "So you forfeit?"

"No," Mike said. "I mean that we, the two of us, me and you are done."

Mike took a breath. He expected an argument, because Val always argued with him, which was fine. But she didn't say anything, so he laid out his evidence as he'd rehearsed this morning.

"The guy's a nut job. I don't know what his deal is, but there's something definitely fucked about him. Like the way he won't let either of us come near him. Not near him like, hey, I'm just gonna stand next to you here—come to think of it, he probably wouldn't let us do that. But like how he jerks away every time you try to touch him. And I think you might actually be sending him the wrong vibes or something, 'cause the way he was looking at you—"

"You jealous?"

Mike had been pacing around, agitated, but now he stopped, faced her. "No-oo," he said. He'd already gotten off track from his speech, and now he couldn't remember what he was supposed to say next.

Val sat back in her chair, ostentatiously crossing one leg over the other. "Are you sure? Because that's totally something a boyfriend would say."

Mike threw his hands up into the air, his mouth open to deny it and continue with his argument, but then the elevator dinged, the doors opening to reveal Clarence. Mike lowered his arms and frowned.

"Hey Clarence," Val said, her voice a cheerful falsetto. "Here he is, Mike. Go ahead and tell him."

"Wait—what?"

Clarence stepped out of the elevator, jumping forward when the doors started to close. He looked expectantly back and forth between the two.

"Well," Val said, "you wanted a chance to apologize, and here it is."

Mike sputtered, unable to find the words. He wanted to forfeit, call her a bitch, tell Clarence he was fucked in the head, go give the finger to Mr. Caruthers, go home and get drunk and never see any of these people again. But a part of him—that deep-seated competitiveness that wanted revenge because she refused to play pool with him anymore because she said she was tired of losing—tightened his stomach and straightened his back as he locked eyes with Clarence.

Through clenched teeth, he said, "I just wanted to say, I'm sorry." His mind raced with something to apologize for, came up empty. "You know, last night—when I drink, I kinda… And I don't want you to get the wrong impression of me…" Fuck, that was the best he could do, and both he and Val knew it. He wasn't good on the spot, and she knew it. "So, we cool?"

Clarence honestly didn't know what Mike had just said, why he was apologizing. He looked at Val, but she was no help for context. She had her hand over her mouth like she was about to cough, but didn't want to ruin the moment. Clarence couldn't think of any reason not to play along.

"Yes," he said. "We, uh—cool."

Val laughed, which made Clarence relax, even as his heart beat a little faster. He smiled at her, but it faded. Mike was scowling at Val, his eyes narrowed. Clarence shuffled his feet, like when he used to walk in on his parents having one of their serious discussions. Because he didn't exist to them in those moments, like he didn't exist to Mike and Val now. It felt uncomfortably familiar.

"I'm, uh—going to get started in the bathrooms," Clarence said.

"Yeah, okay," Val said. "We'll get started in the offices, then."

"Okay," Clarence mumbled and shuffled off.

Once the bathroom door had closed behind him, Mike bent over at the waist and got in Val's face.

"It's on." He shook his finger at her, her smile still in place, irritating him even more. "It's fucking on! You're going down!"

"Maybe," she said, tipping him a wink. "We'll see."

Mike's mouth dropped open and he straightened, blinked. Val rose from her chair and brushed by him, didn't touch him, but didn't touch him in that special way that girls had of not touching guys. Mike's head spun as he followed her down the hallway to the first office.

The office building felt completely different in the afternoon, with the sun still shining in the windows. Mike and Val played Vampire, avoiding the beams of sunlight that angled through the windows. After Clarence was done with the bathrooms, they tried to get him to be the Vampire Hunter, but he declined, turning away slowly. So Val volunteered to be the hunter and Mike and Clarence could be the vampires. Clarence agreed to that and even laughed a little as he dodged away from Val's duster-turned-stake.

Mike allowed himself to be caught. Val knew that he had thrown the game, but had a better poker face, so Mike thought he was being clever. Val pushed the handle of the duster against Mike's chest over his heart. He put his hand on hers, as if driving the stake deeper and looked into her eyes, not with hammed up death agony, but with a little half-smile. Val's satisfied smirk belonged to the huntress. Clarence sprayed the office's desk with Pledge and wiped it down, keeping a wary eye on Val, lest she turn her attention and catch him off-guard.

The three of them came out of the office laughing, Clarence shutting the door and wiping the handle clean behind them. They hadn't heard the stairwell door while in the office, their laughter clogging in their throats at the sight of Mr. Caruthers standing with his arms folded, seeming to fill the hallway.

"What the hell are you three doing?"

Mike and Val took a step away from each other and Clarence looked down at his feet.

Before Mike or Val could come up with some kind of excuse, Clarence blurted, "I'm sorry, sir. We were playing a game."

"Yeah?" Mr. Caruthers said. "You having fun?"

Confused, Clarence looked at Mike, who shook his head slightly. But Clarence didn't get the message that he shouldn't say anything.

"I'm sorry sir," he said, guilt tightening his throat. "It won't happen again. I promise."

"It's not his fault!" Val said, stepping forward, almost shielding Clarence.

"Yeah!" Mike said, stepping in front of her. "I started fooling around and Val and Clarence were just humoring me." Realizing that he was apologizing to his prick of a boss, an apology that he'd been forced into by Clarence, then Val, put an edge in his voice. "You know how much I like to make a jackass of myself," he said, using Mr. Caruthers's words.

"Yeah. I do." Mr. Caruthers turned to Clarence, who was looking over Val's shoulder. "Clarence, I'm disappointed in you. I'm counting on you to keep these two in line. Now get to it!" He checked his watch. "It's quarter to two and you're still on the sixth."

Tears stung Clarence's eyes, his chin lowering to his chest and his glasses sliding down his nose. His stomach felt heavy and twisted. Movement caught his peripheral vision and he looked up in time to see Val giving the finger to the closing stairwell door, Mike yanking at his crotch.

Clarence jumped around them, glancing up at the security camera. "No, stop! He'll see and you'll get in trouble!"

"Oh, please," Val said, even though she lowered her finger. "That asshole may be a creeper, but he's not gonna rewind the tapes to see every single thing we do."

"Yeah," Mike agreed. "He only checks up on us often enough to be a prick. And he can't get his fat ass downstairs that quick." Mike walked over to the lobby chairs. "We probably got a good ten minutes before he's back in front of his stupid monitors."

Val joined him, sliding down in another chair and putting her feet up on the coffee table. Clarence winced. He'd just cleaned the lobby furniture.

"I think we should get back to work," he said. "Mr. Caruthers is right. We are kind of behind now." To himself, he said, "I'm so stupid."

Val heard him and jumped up. "Don't say that! He's an asshole." A smile stretching her face, she sang, "A! S-S! H-O! L-E! Everybody!"

"A! S-S! H-O! L-E!" Mike sang.

Mike started grunting in the same rhythm and Val expected Clarence to smile. He still frowned, though, so she put her feet on the floor and pushed herself up. Mike looked up at her for a second, then rolled his eyes and also stood.

They crossed the lobby to clean the offices on the east side of the building, which meant that there weren't any squares of setting sun on the carpet to dodge. Their mood was darker, and they cleaned the first two offices on that side in silence, Mike and Val letting Clarence linger with his sprays and wipes since he seemed to have a lot on his mind.

Clarence had let himself relax. When he'd come back from cleaning the bathrooms, they'd told him about the game they were playing and instead of reminding them that they were there to work, he'd played along, just because they'd reminded him of Mickey, how he had looked in Clarence's dream, so mischievous and happy. It served him right, getting yelled at like that.

Clarence vigorously scrubbed the air vent, the ammonia and his tears making his eyes sting.

When he came out of the office, wiping the doorknob clean, Mike and Val were standing there. Mike had his arms folded and Val had her hand on his shoulder, a concerned expression on her face and her mouth open like she'd just been saying something to Mike. His scowl deepened when he saw Clarence, who blushed and shuffled his feet.

"Clarence, what the hell—"

"Don't listen to him," Val said, shooting an elbow into Mike's side.

He grunted and cradled his ribs, his jaw clenching. Stepping forward, Val stopped just short of putting her hand on Clarence's arm when he stepped away from her.

"You know," she continued, "he's got no right to make you feel that way."

"Who? What?" Clarence looked at Mike.

"Oh, come on, Clarence," she said, exasperated, gesturing toward the stairwell. "I saw your face when he yelled at you! Why did you let him talk to you like that?"

"I don't know. I..." Clarence fought the urge to take the Purell out of his pocket and sanitize. Instead, he touched the bottle through his Dockers and felt a little better. He shrugged. "I don't know."

This was ridiculous. Mike had to do something to end this stupid fucking game once and for all. He couldn't just tackle Clarence and steal a five, Val would call foul. But if they didn't work with him anymore, then it would be over and things could go back to the way they'd been. Or even better, he and Val could screw around in the bathroom instead of playing games.

Val opened her mouth to say something else, but Mike overrode her. "Dude, you can't just take that shit! You gotta get back at him!"

Clarence's face blanched. "What? No. No, I can't—" he choked on the words, sputtered, ""get back at him"."

"Well, you gotta do something!" Mike said, warming up to this now that he saw Val nodding along. "I mean, you don't have to, like, punch him in the face or anything. Just, you know, something to show him he can't just fuck with you whenever he wants." Clarence was still pallid, but seemed willing to listen, so Mike started pacing, getting into it. "Like, I don't know. Shit!" he snatched his key ring from his belt, flipping through them. "Do we have keys to the stairwell doors? That'd be fucking hilarious!"

"Don't be stupid," Val snapped. "If we have keys, so does he. And, we're the only ones in the building. He'd know it was us."

"Son of a bitch!"

"That's probably true for anything we could think of," Clarence murmured. He glanced up at the security camera that felt like it was pointed right at him. "Are we done up here? Can we go down to five?"

Val's lips tightened down into a thin line, holding back what she wanted to say. She nodded, picked up her stuff and headed to the elevator. Mike stood, his arms still in the air from his wild waving, his mouth hanging open. He gaped at Clarence who broke eye contact. Then, swearing more or less under his breath, he grabbed the vacuum and followed Val. Clarence brought up the rear with the cart.

At the elevator, he nodded at the cart and said, "You go on ahead."

Val sighed and Mike scowled.

In the elevator, Clarence allowed himself to feel a little thrilled at the thought of getting back at Mr. Caruthers, the same thrill as when he'd considered not cleaning the office doorframe after he'd touched it. It scared Clarence… but still. He didn't like when Mr. Caruthers yelled at him. Rationally, he knew it was his fault, he deserved it, but there was a childish part inside that wanted to hurt Mr. Caruthers because he'd hurt him first.

Clarence had been an only child, and his friend, Mickey was the closest he'd ever had to a brother. When they'd been eight, Mickey had come home from a two week stay with his cousins, and he'd learned a great game called Two for Flinching. Of course, Clarence had flinched and Mickey had hit him twice in the shoulder, hard. Pissed off, Clarence had kicked him in the nuts and punched him in the face. Mickey had run home crying, then his mom had called Clarence's mom, and after hearing what had happened, assured her that there would be an immediate apology. Before that, she sat Clarence down on the couch, shooed his father out of the room, and sat next to him.

"Clarence, you shouldn't hit people."

"But he—!"

"I know," his mother soothed. "I know. But that doesn't mean that it was okay for you to hit him. If someone hits you or hurts your feelings, and it's more than just roughhousing, because I know how boys like to roughhouse. I grew up with three brothers." She stopped, getting herself back on track. "I mean, if someone is making you feel bad, just get out of there. Come find me, find a teacher, find the parent, or coach, or whoever's supposed to be in charge, and you tell them what happened. That's what your father and I do, except we go to people called the police. They stop people who hurt other people."

Clarence didn't say anything, still staring at his feet.

"Do you understand?"

Clarence nodded, then looked up. "Mom, being in trouble makes me feel bad."

She blinked twice, eyes wide, then she burst out laughing. She hugged him. "Your father and I don't count, Clarence. We're trying to teach you lessons, not make you feel bad. You should be excited to learn something new."

Clarence hadn't felt very excited, but had taken the lesson to heart, so when the elevator doors opened onto the fifth floor, he had only a small, lingering butterfly in his stomach at the thought of retaliating against Mr. Caruthers.

But Mike wasn't letting it go.

"We could lock him in his office."

"He has keys," Val sighed. "And he'd fire us."

Mike tilted a chair back while Clarence ran his Dyson under it. He talk-shouted, "We could lock him out of his office."

"Keys. Fired."

"Lock him out of the building."

"That's so lame. He's so got keys and we'd so be fired!" Val dumped the small garbage can into the big bag she held, slamming the can back down onto the floor.

Mike looked sheepish, his lips pursed and his nostrils flaring as he filtered his ideas. "We could… mess with his lunch… somehow."

"Again!" Val stomped her foot. "He'd know it was us!"

"We could mess with his lunch like he didn't know there was anything wrong with it," Mike said, a lapdog grin on his face.

"And how do we do that?"

Clarence felt sick to his stomach. Every time Mike suggested something, Clarence's heart skipped a beat and he felt thrilled, upset that he was even considering it, giddy that he had friends that wanted to help him out, and guilty because it was his fault they'd been yelled at and now they'd been dragged into it. He tried to pretend that he didn't hear Mike over the vacuum, but it was obvious that he could since Val did.

"I—don't know…" Mike trailed off, almost letting the bookcase that he was moving tip over. Val dusted behind it, and Mike almost shouted into her face, "We could fart-salad him!"

"Mike—"

"See?" he said, turning to Clarence and almost tipping the bookcase over again. "He always has a salad for lunch—it's a wonder he's so fucking fat. So it's kinda like a fart-pillow. You fart on someone's pillow, and then when they go to bed, they get a great big face-full!" He started laughing.

Val stopped dusting, put a fist on her hip. "I don't know why you're single, you charmer."

Sneering, he said, "Alright, smart ass. Got any better ideas?"

Val didn't, but then her eyes sharpened and she opened her mouth.

Before she could say anything, Clarence said, "What's the point?"

Mike and Val turned to look at him, almost as if they'd forgotten he was there.

"So we fart-salad him." Clarence shuddered. "He wouldn't know it was us getting back at him. So what do we do, laugh at him behind his back? My mom taught me that's wrong." He swallowed the lump in his throat. "She also taught me that getting back at people is wrong. She said I should tell someone in charge, and since Mr. Caruthers is in charge, I can't do anything about it."

Mike stood, stunned. Then, he threw his hands up in the air, seizing the bookcase as it started to overbalance. The guy was fucking hopeless.

Val's eyes welled up. She walked over to Clarence, stopping at a respectful distance. "Did your mom ever make you feel bad?"

Clarence nodded. "Sometimes. But she said it didn't count, because she was trying to teach me, not make me feel bad."

Val nodded, and took another step closer. "Do you think Mr. Caruthers is trying to teach you?"

Mike leaned forward. Val had that look in her eye. He closed his eyes for a moment, just wanting this sideshow therapy session to be over.

"I don't—I mean, yes," Clarence said. "I was in charge, and I wasn't doing my job—"

"How you figure you're in charge?" Mike interrupted.

"I've been here the longest," Clarence said. "And I'm older than you, both of you. I should've known better, like Mr. Caruthers said."

"No," Val said, taking another step. Clarence didn't shy away, and she continued, "Mr. Caruthers is not a teacher. He's a bully." She fixed Clarence with a hard stare. "And you're not a kid anymore. You can't be crying to mama when a bully beats you down. You got to stand up to him."

Clarence became aware of how close Val was. His first instinct was to move away, but then he didn't. Her presence comforted him, and if he breathed shallowly, the germs on his breath would shrivel in the air before they reached her and he could catch just a whiff of her body wash. It was intoxicating.

Also, it was dangerous. Clarence didn't jerk away, but he took a deliberate step back and Val didn't follow.

Mike let out the breath he'd been holding.

"So what do you want to do?" Val asked.

Clarence turned off the Dyson. He bowed his head to have time to consider. He tried to think about what Mr. Caruthers had taught him, and couldn't think of anything. Clarence raised his head, made eye contact with Val, then Mike, back to Val. He nodded and Val smiled. Mike still looked confused.

"The security cameras," Clarence said, smiling for the first time in a long time.

He'd been thinking about it for the last hour, while Mike came up with one lame plan after another. The source of the problem was also the solution.

"Well," he explained, "Mr. Caruthers watches us. Not constantly, but he checks often enough to know—when we're slacking off."

"Dude," Mike said.

"I know, I know," Clarence shook his head. "He checks up on us, and when he sees something he doesn't like, he comes to yell at us. What if—" he held up a finger, "he didn't see us at all?"

"Like, take out the cameras?" Mike asked.

Val twisted her lip in thought. "No, I think I see where he's going with this." Turning to Clarence, she asked, "So, we hide in the offices, then let him come and yell at us?"

"Kind of," Clarence replied. "One of us will stay in the stairwell. The other two will clean the offices we can get to without being seen. Mr. Caruthers won't see us, so he'll come looking. He always takes the stairs, so the one of us in the stairwell will hear him—"

"Comes out, joins the others—" Val joined in.

"By the time he finds us," Mike said, practically jumping up and down, "we're all working like nothing's up. Holy shit!" He would've clapped Clarence on the back if he hadn't been standing across the room. "You're a mad genius!"

Clarence blushed, his scalp showing pink through his thin blonde hair.

"It's fucking brilliant!" Val said, grinning widely. "It'll drive him fucking nuts! But—!" She pointed a serious finger at Mike, then Clarence, then back and forth between them with each word. "You two need to work on your poker faces. One giggle." She pointed at Mike. "One guilty look." She pointed at Clarence, who tried desperately not to dip his head. "And we're in some serious trouble. Like, fired kind of trouble."

Mike and Clarence both nodded solemnly.

"Alright!" Val cheered.

Mike fist-pumped the air.

Clarence gripped his thighs, his palms sweating lightly.

Val decided that she should be in the stairwell. She had the speed and subtlety to join them in the office quickly without making any noise. Plus, Clarence knew the cameras like the back of his hand. Staying late so many times had forced him to know where the cameras pointed so he could avoid them as much as possible, hoping to appear as only a shifting shadow when he'd needed to cross one's sightline.

"Yeah, how'd that work out for you?" Mike asked.

"Don't be a prick," Val said, then punched Mike in the arm.

Mike held his arm and sulked. Designated as the muscle, he moved furniture out of the way for Clarence and helped clean.

The two men were cleaning the last office that Clarence thought they'd be able to get to without passing in front of any cameras when Val rushed in, out of breath and grinning.

"Coming! He's coming!"

Mike turned to Clarence, who said, "Now. Mike in Mr. Carlisle's office, Val in Mr. Tanaka's. I'll take Mrs. Fleur's."

The three split up, rushing across the hall. Clarence's heart hammered and he was sweating profusely, half from the hard work, half from nerves. He kept his eyes forward, focused on what he was doing, and resisted the urge to look over his shoulder. Glancing over his shoulder would make him look guilty, Mike had said. So he cleaned and kept cleaning, even when his glasses slid so far down his nose that he needed to tilt his head back to be able to see anything.

His focus was so tight that when he turned around to get another roll of paper towel off his cart and saw Mr. Caruthers standing there, he jumped.

Mr. Caruthers watched Clarence's face

carefully, right hand absently rubbing his left arm. Clarence had given no indication that he'd realized that his boss was in the room. Now that he had, he was acting strange. Mr. Caruthers couldn't figure it out at first, then he got it. Clarence was making eye contact, not ducking his head or looking away or hunching his shoulders or any of the things that Clarence usually did when Mr. Caruthers was around.

Clarence started to feel nervous with his boss standing there, staring at him.

"Can I do something for you, sir?"

Mr. Caruthers narrowed his eyes, then replied, "How long're you planning to stay up here on five?" He expected Clarence to act chagrinned.

Clarence didn't break eye contact. "We're just about done up here, sir."

Mr. Caruthers grunted. Then, he stomped away.

"What the fuck?" Mr. Caruthers said to himself, taking it slow down the stairs.

He sat down to take a break between floors four and three, then again between two and one. Reaching his office, he fell into his chair and stared at the paperwork on his desk. Glancing up at one of the monitors, he saw the trio waiting for the elevator to go down to four. His eyebrows lowered and he pursed his lips, thinking.

Mr. Caruthers tried to focus. Tibble & Shuster on four was requesting softer toilet paper in their fax machine.

No, that wasn't right.

Mr. Caruthers swore. Someone on four had sent

the office supply requisition to the wrong person, and it was obvious where Tibble & Shuster wanted more toilet paper. Mr. Caruthers leaned back in his chair and stared at the monitors.

There they were, up on four, mouths moving, talking to each other, moving at a decent clip. They'd probably be done on time, even with all their messing around.

Mr. Caruthers sighed and leaned back over the paperwork.

"No," Clarence said, once they were on the fourth floor and Mike suggested that they hide again.

"Yeah," Val chimed in, which irritated Mike. "He's probably watching us right now, thinking that something's up."

"Yeah," Clarence said, and Mike definitely didn't like how he smiled at Val, inched closer to her. "We need to lull him into a false sense of security. We'll stay where he can see us for a little bit, then disappear one by one." He looked down the hall, tilting his eyes, but not his head to look up at the cameras. "Let's start on this side, then move over to the other side. Then, we can get under the cameras again."

Val grinned. Mike could only manage a tight-lipped smile.

Mr. Caruthers hit 'send' in his email and leaned back in his chair. It was a simple concept. He could act as supply manager for any company that rented space in the building, for a managerial fee, of course. If a company didn't pony up, they were responsible for their own office supplies, including fax machine paper.

It was a simple concept, but seemed beyond the intellectual capabilities of Mr. Tanager, the office manager on two, who was always trying to mooch supplies off Mr. Caruthers, because he knew he had them.

The email had been carefully crafted. On the surface, it reiterated how the arrangement worked. Between the lines, Mr. Caruthers told Mr. Tanager to go fuck himself.

The smile that had started to form, imagining the look on that skinny little prick's face when he read the email, felt slapped off when Mr. Caruthers glanced at the monitors, watched them for a minute, two, five.

Mike, Val and Clarence had disappeared again.

"What the fuck?" he demanded, drawing out the last word as he heaved himself up out of his chair.

The next time it happened, Mr. Caruthers pulled up the stored file on the computer and watched it like a hawk, from the moment he saw himself walking back toward the stairwell on four up to when he saw himself walking through the halls on three, looking for them again. It didn't make any sense. One minute they were there, the next they weren't.

Mr. Caruthers breathed heavily as he watched the footage, his hands cold and clammy.

"Let's not do it on this floor," Val said in the elevator, she and Mike on their way down to two.

Mike couldn't stop laughing. "Why? This is fucking hilarious! Did you see his face?" He puffed his cheeks out and held his breath until he turned bright red. Then, he sputtered laughter again.

"Exactly," Val said. "He's getting pissed because he's suspicious."

Mike took a moment to consider, then nodded. "You're a pretty smart cookie."

Val dropped him a wink just as the elevator door opened, then brushed by him.

Mr. Caruthers watched them scurry around on the second floor. Looking at his watch, he saw they only had two hours to go. Two floors in two hours.

He leaned back in his chair, raised his coffee to his lips. "Finally decided to stop fucking around, huh?" he asked the figures on the screen.

"Hey guys," Clarence said, looking at this watch as they were finishing up on two. "We only have about fifty minutes to clean the building's lobby. I think we've messed with him enough."

"You know what they say," Mike said, half-disappointed, half-still-excited. "Enough is never enough."

"No, I think that Clarence is right," Val said for what felt like the thousandth time that afternoon.

Mike rolled his eyes.

"Besides," Clarence said. "I have an idea that'll really drive him nuts."

Clarence smiled, and Mike had a moment to think about how Clarence looked when he smiled. His whole face seemed drawn up, pinched together, tight and fragile, it was like his smile had broken his face. The fluorescent light flashing off Clarence's glasses as he looked back and forth between Mike and Val, he looked more than a little unsettled and unsettling.

"Let's clean his office!" Clarence said, wringing his hands together, eyes and smile wide.

Mike and Val looked at each other. Mike felt unsure, wondering what Clarence's definition of funny actually was, when Val started laughing.

"Uhh…" he said when Val doubled over, holding her stomach. "Can I buy a vowel?"

Val shook her head and held up a finger, still laughing. Mike felt left out, which pissed him off because Val was his friend; he'd known her for way longer, had put in the time, and if anyone got to sleep with her, it should be him.

They finished cleaning the building's lobby a few minutes before six. Clarence was coiling up the cord of his Dyson, wiping it with a Clorox Wipe as he went, Mike was moving furniture back into place and Val was coming out of the bathroom when Mr. Caruthers came out of the stairwell. He didn't look too out of breath, but his face was white, except for two hot spots on his cheek and one on his forehead.

"You guys are done," he said between puffing breaths.

"Yeah, we're done," Mike said.

"That wasn't a question," Mr. Caruthers said, one hand on his stomach, the other a fist on where his waist should be. "I meant, it's six o' clock, and you're done."

"Yeah," Mike repeated, rolling his eyes. "We're done.

"No, no. I only want to hear one thing from you. And that's…"

Mike wouldn't say it. Val was too far away, not a part of the conversation. Mike closed his eyes, prayed that Clarence wouldn't say—

"Yes, sir," he said.

Mike groaned.

"That's what I thought," Mr. Caruthers said.

He turned away, smiling, dominance reasserted. Mike looked at Clarence, expecting his usual sheepish expression and downcast eyes, but he stared at Mr. Caruthers with a little smile on his face. Mike shuddered.

After the three of them had punched out, they walked out of the building together. Clarence couldn't help looking over his shoulder at his boss, who was locking the building's main door behind them. He'd go down to his office, and then come back out through the service entrance on the far side of the building in less than ten minutes. Clarence knew his routine almost as well as he knew his own.

Facing forward again, he said, "Twenty minutes. You're coming back, right?"

"Totally," Val said, struggling not to laugh.

"Okay, twenty minutes," Clarence said, a flutter in his stomach.

As they walked away, he heard Mike say, "I'm missing something."

Whether Val told him or not, Clarence didn't know; they were out of earshot. It didn't matter anyway. What mattered is if they came back. He got into his car, sanitizing the handle behind him, and drove out of the parking lot. He thought about parking a couple buildings down the service drive, but then worried that Mr. Caruthers might see his car as he drove past and get suspicious. Then, he crossed the freeway and was going to park a few buildings up the service drive, but then he found he couldn't sit still. He was too excited and nervous. He turned onto Evergreen heading south, drove for five minutes, then turned around. He pulled back into the parking lot of the Haimes Building, exactly twenty minutes after leaving it. Mr. Caruthers' car was nowhere to be seen.

Neither was Mike's blue Toyota.

Clarence tried to shrug it off, but then it was half an hour, forty minutes. At fifty-three minutes, a blue Toyota pulled into the empty parking lot, and Clarence's eyes welled up. He just couldn't believe it.

He had friends!

Mike didn't seem like he shared the sentiment though.

He and Val had driven around for almost an hour while he tried to pry out of her why cleaning Mr. Caruthers' office was going to be so funny. Instead of telling him, each time, she just laughed. It started pissing him off even worse when he suspected that she was forcing her laughter just to fuck with him.

Clarence's smile faded as soon as he saw Mike's face.

"It'll be funny," Clarence assured him. "You'll see." When Mike's expression didn't change, he said, "I promise."

It took about five minutes cleaning Mr. Caruthers' office and Clarence's specific instructions to put things back exactly where they'd been for Mike to start to get it. The first thing he did was to clean the desk top, which had been dust-covered except for a swath of use. As he carefully put the stapler, the phone, the desk lamp, all also clean now, back in their places, he realized how different the desk looked, even though it was exactly the same.

"Just clean," Mike finished out loud. Turning to Clarence, he said, "You're a mad genius."

"Finally figured it out, huh?" Val asked, her smirk cute and irritating at the same time.

"Yeah, yeah, stupid Mike," he said.

Clarence grinned at the two of them.

It took them about half an hour to clean the office, all three of them laughing practically the whole time. On their way out of the building, Clarence still giving them plenty of room, Val stopped short. Clarence didn't yelp in surprise or fear, but he skidded to a halt.

"Coming to the bar with us, C?" she asked like it was no big deal.

"Not tonight," he answered, also like it was no big deal. Then, before he had a chance to think about it, he asked, "You guys want to come over to my place tomorrow? We could—"

What did people do when they got together on Sunday?

"Yeah!" Mike jumped on it. "The Lions don't look like a complete train wreck this year. Five o'clock cool?"

"Yes, of course," Clarence said, wondering if

Barry Sanders was still on the team.

"Cool," Val said.

After Clarence had gotten into his car and driven away, Mike turned to Val and said, "Alright, sudden death."

"It was always sudden death," she said after a moment, almost forgetting that they were supposed to be battling for the championship of the universe.

"I mean, it's tomorrow or nothing. I've had it with his "don't-get-too-close-I-might-explode" whatever thing that's his problem."

"Oh come on, I had fun today. You did too."

"Yeah, alright, it was fun. But I'm seriously worried about what would happen if we spend too much more time pretending to be his friend."

"What? You worried we might actually become his friends?"

Mike stared at her over the top of the car, then got in. "No. I'm worried he might think you two are becoming…"

Val let it hang between them for a count of twenty, just to watch Mike squirm a little. Then, she smiled.

"Well, if it's sudden death, we gotta raise the stakes."

"Name it," he said.

"Whoever wins, the other does whatever they want."

Mike licked his lips. He liked the sound of that.

"What if we both want the same thing?" he asked.

His breath caught in his throat. It was as close as he'd ever come to asking Val point blank how she felt about him.

She looked at him with that smirk she had that made him want to kiss her and choke her at the same time.

"Guess we'll see."

13

Clarence had shown her that it could be done, so Lucy stood at the sliding glass door that had once looked out at the apartments' courtyard, the apple tree growing in the middle of it. The fog seemed to press against the glass, wanting inside, to get her. She closed her eyes, concentrating. The tree leaves, green in the spring, orange and yellow in the fall, the bark a muted gray brown. She tried to remember the way the bark of the tree she'd climbed with Clarence had felt against her skin. She could almost hear the leaves rustling in the breeze.

She heard them! Lucy opened her eyes and there was the tree, in sunlight that spilled through the patio door, warming her.

She squealed in delight, clapping a hand over her mouth and peeking toward her mother's bedroom. There was no sound, no indication that she'd been heard. She quietly unlocked the patio door, slid it open. She crept out onto the patio, closed her eyes, ready to savor the feeling of the grass beneath her bare feet. She stepped forward.

Lucy stopped, looked down. The grass felt like shaggy carpet and gray fog puffed out when she took another step. Beyond the tree, the grass, and the parking lot was gray fog, inching closer.

She took a step back onto the patio and tried to calm herself. Clarence had broken her mother's magic so easily. She tried to focus on the rustling of the leaves, the wind blowing. She whispered words, not knowing where the magical chant came from, raising her hands to ward off the approaching fog.

Sure that the spell must have worked, she opened her eyes, let her hands fall and yelped. The fog rushed toward her, making a low growling sound, growing louder as it got closer. Gray nothingness enveloped the tree and Lucy sprang backward through the glass door, sliding it shut behind her. The gray fog cascaded up, obliterating even the patio.

Lucy stood panting, bracing herself against the glass. She raced over to peek around the corner at the door of her mother's bedroom, but there was still no sign that she'd heard Lucy trying to escape. Frustrated and scared, Lucy started crying.

A breath of wind, like the last sigh of consciousness before sleep, tickled the small hairs around her ears and she felt him in the living room behind her.

"Lucy!" Clarence called, seeing her by the hallway. Her wet, black hair clung to her neck like a leech, her pale skin glowing mutely in the nowhere light of the apartment. Remembering the game, he held a hand up to his mouth, then bowed. "M'lady! What is your pleasure today?"

Lucy straightened, but hung her head. She'd wanted to see him again, for him to come back, but now his presence just reminded her of what had happened the last time he'd come to play.

"Lucy?" Clarence asked, concern raising his

voice. "What's wrong?"

Not looking at him and without a word, she walked down the hallway to her bedroom. Clarence followed, stumbled over nothing on the floor near the kitchen. He inspected the empty air, wondering what he'd touched and if he should clean it, although he didn't think it was that important if what he touched was nothing, when he heard the soft click of Lucy's door shutting. He hurried down the hall and tapped on it, reaching into his pocket for a Lysol wipe, but found his pockets empty. Oddly, that's not what concerned him at the moment.

"Lucy?" he called, opening the door slowly.

She sat in the middle of the floor, her chin resting on her knees. Her wet hair hung in tendrils and her shoulders twitched up and down as she cried.

Clarence went to her timidly, squatted by her side. He reached out and, after a moment's hesitation, lightly touched her shoulder. When she didn't immediately start coughing blood, he squeezed her shoulder in what he hoped was a reassuring way, tucked a lock of dripping hair behind her ear so he could see her face. Her eyes flicked to him out of their corners, then she turned away.

"Lucy, what's wrong?" Clarence blinked and sat up, puzzled. The last time he saw her, they'd been playing at the park in the neighborhood where he'd grown up. He'd told her about his mom, the way she died, and then… what?

"Did my story about my mom scare you?"

When she didn't reply, he thought a little more.

"Were you mad at Mickey? We're best friends, spit brothers. I could ask him to apologize."

Still no answer.

"Does your mom not like me?" He tried to remember what she'd said. "You said she was mad at you."

Lucy pulled herself a little tighter, the lock of hair that Clarence had tucked behind her ear falling free and Clarence turned away, squeezing his eyes shut against the memory of his mom.

Finally, he asked the first thing that he'd thought, what he hoped wouldn't get an answer. "Are you mad at me?"

Lucy dipped her head a little lower, pressing her mouth against her folded arms and said, "You left me."

Clarence was taken aback. "No! I, uh—my mom must have called me to come in, right? I told you I'd come back to play soon and I am. Back. To, uh—play."

Lucy turned to him, confusion squeezing more tears out of her eyes. "Why are you such a liar? You were in bed, sick, and your mom was taking care of you. Then, there was some horrible noise and you screamed and disappeared, then everything disappeared, and I was lost in the fog." She pulled herself back into a ball. "Then I was here again."

"I—what?" Clarence's brow wrinkled. "Wait. We were playing at the park. With Mickey. I haven't seen him in…" Clarence stood, looking around for a mirror. "How old am I?"

The question caught Lucy off guard and she stopped crying, was about to answer, when Clarence grabbed her shoulders.

"Wait. Did I tell you about my dream?" He looked away, lost in thought. "I was with you in the park, playing with Mickey, and then mom called me in, I told you I'd come back and play, and then I woke up because I had a nightmare about—No!"

Clarence jerked away from her, then lunged forward. He grabbed her by the shoulders and shook her once, hard. "What's going on?"

Then he saw her, small and scared, her eyes wide and her lower lip trembling. His heart broke with remorse and he tried to hug her, to apologize, but she pushed him away, stronger than he would have expected from such a skinny-limbed girl.

"No! I don't want to be your friend anymore, Clarence!" He stood up and backed away from her and she rose, angry for the first time and unsure of what to do. She wanted to hit him and cry at the same time. Her fist clenched at her sides, she struggled for what to say or do. Finally, she screamed, "I'm not going to think of you when I hug Ducky anymore! I hope Ducky turns into a prince that's not you because you're not a prince, not a real one!" Then, she fell to her knees, crying again, sobbing.

Clarence took an unsure step toward her, then stopped. Because she wasn't really there. He wasn't really here. This was his apartment, his reading room, but instead of his recliner and his books and Monet on the walls – here was a bed, a child-sized desk and some picture books strewn around on the floor. It wasn't even his bedroom from when he was a child. He'd had posters on all four walls, cats with bad hair days and Footloose and Transformers and G.I. Joes. These walls were empty, sad.

So he wasn't in his apartment, and he wasn't in his bedroom at his parents' house. He wandered around the room, touching the walls, picking things up and absent-mindedly tidying up.

"It looks like my apartment." He stopped what he was doing to look at Lucy, who wasn't crying now, but watching Clarence. "This is your room?"

She nodded.

"Hmm," he grunted, putting a SpongeBob SquarePants with a McDonald's 'M' stamped on its foot back onto the shelf. "I guess maybe…"

He'd paced the room twice, and started on a third trip, trailing his fingers along the wall. Then he paused. Clarence turned. Lucy couldn't see what had made him stop. Then Clarence rushed out of the room, across the hall to the bathroom.

Lucy squeezed her hands together, listening for the crunch of broken glass under his feet, wanted to breathe easier when she just heard the faucet running, but couldn't. She followed and stood in the bathroom's doorway.

Clarence hunched over the sink, watching the water run down the drain. After about a minute, he held his hand over the drain, which gurgled. He shut the faucet off and let the water run down, then he went to the tub. Lucy's heart beat harder as he bent over, putting his face near the drain.

"“Hello? Can you hear me?”

Lucy giggled. “Of course I can hear you, silly.”

Clarence shot to his feet like she’d scared him. He pushed his fists into his mouth and seemed about to scream, except he couldn’t breathe. He’d touched her. Put his hand on her shoulder. Touched her things, her toys, her books. He’d washed none of it. His heart pounded in his ears. He twisted his body around hers to get to the sink. He needed to wash his hands now, but his Lysol Hands-Free Soap Dispenser wasn’t there. Clarence leaned this way and that, looking for it amid the clutter of make-up, Colgate and Colgate Kids, and an electric razor that wasn’t his and fuck the hands-free dispenser, any soap would do! He turned the knob for the hot water as far as it would go, but nothing came out.

“This is a nightmare,” he groaned when the shower’s faucet didn’t work either. He brushed past Lucy who followed him to the kitchen to another malfunctioning sink.

Clarence’s vision was getting spotty from lack of oxygen and he held onto the counter to keep from losing his balance and everything was so unreal, like his worst dream come true.

“Wait,” he wheezed. “This is a nightmare.” The knowledge didn’t seem to help soothe him. Except he realized that he hadn’t been breathing for minutes now and wasn’t really suffering. Only thought that he was suffering because he thought he should be.

“Does that make any sense?” Clarence asked

Lucy, who was peeking around the corner at him. Her eyes widened and she shook her head. He grunted again.

Clarence walked to the sliding glass door, saw the apple tree, the lawn, the parking lot, but before he saw all those things, he saw gray fog receding, like it was being pushed back as he walked forward.

Lucy crept up beside him, looking back and forth between Clarence and the world outside that he'd brought into existence.

"How do you do that?" she whispered.

"Do what?"

"The fog. The queen destroyed the world."

"The—who?" Clarence raised a hand, held his forehead. "What now?"

"I tried," Lucy said. "I stood right where you are, and I tried so hard to see the tree, the grass, the things I remembered. I saw them, but when I went outside, the fog came back."

The tree stood about a dozen feet from the door, grass between it and his patio. Another few feet of grass stood between the tree and the parking lot. On the other side of that was Outer Drive, and the houses across the street, not the vibrant colors he remembered, but gray around the edges, wispy, fading into pencil line detail as he looked down the street.

"I don't know," he said truthfully.

Lucy's small, hopeful smile faded. They went back to looking out the window. Clarence didn't want to ask the questions that he had, afraid of the answers; Lucy wanted to go outside, but was afraid that the fog would try to rush in on her again, and this time she'd be lost for good. She thought she heard something behind her, like the soft purring of a piece of paper being torn in half, but the living room was empty. Other than that, the apartment was silent.

"What do you dream about?" Clarence finally asked.

Lucy's brow wrinkled as she thought. Clarence smiled at such a serious expression on her young face, but then became serious again when she took longer to answer than expected.

"I don't dream." She crossed her arms and pouted.

"Really? I used to dream a lot as a kid. Still do actually…"

"So?" Lucy stomped away from the window and sat on the couch. "I told you I don't dream."

"Never?" Mouth twisting to the side in thought, he crossed the room and sat beside her. "You don't dream about Ducky turning into a prince and taking you to live with him in his castle far, far away?"

She didn't answer.

"It's okay to tell me. I won't laugh at you or anything."

Lucy's head hung a little, and she turned to the side so he couldn't see her face.

"Do you ever dream about me?" Then, worried that he sounded like a pedophile to this girl who probably didn't know what that was, he added, "Like, when we played at the park the other day?"

Lucy squeezed her eyes shut, trying to

remember the last time she'd dreamed, the last time she'd gone to bed. The night before she'd broken the bathroom mirror and her mother destroyed the world outside the apartment, she'd dreamed that her daddy and she had gone outside to play under the apple tree because her mom was dead. She'd woken up crying.

"No," she said, hair falling forward to hide her face.

Clarence was silent for a moment, unsure how to proceed. "I think—I think I dream about you."

Lucy looked up at him in surprise.

"I think I dream that you're my friend and we talk. Play." Clarence pushed his glasses up his nose, where they stayed. "I like that I dream about you."

Clarence's hands twisted together in his lap. They were pink, clean, nothing under his nails. Lucy's hands were pale, clammy; there was some greenish crust under all her finger- and toenails. She picked at it every day, but it wouldn't go away.

"Clarence?"

"Yeah?"

"Will you protect me?"

"What?"

"My mother is—" Lucy looked around, leaned in, whispered, "evil. She does bad things to me."

Clarence's heart thumped and his vision clouded a little. Still, he forced his voice to be calm, steady as he asked, "What sort of bad things? She makes you clean, you told me that."

Lucy shook her head. "No. She stood on my feet and pulled on my hands. It hurt a lot. When she makes me clean, I need to pick up the broken glass in the bathroom and it cuts my fingers."

She held out her hands for him to see. He was sure that they'd been fine moments ago, but now they were puckered all over with cuts. His heart skipped a beat, then double-thumped. He wanted to gather Lucy into his arms, tell her it'd be alright. She put her hands back into her lap, and Clarence noticed they were smooth and uncut again. He pulled back from her a little, and Lucy looked up at him quickly.

"Is it because I've been bad?" She wasn't crying; that made it worse. "Mommy says I'm a bad kid and I should grow up and stop being such a little—" her voice dropped "*—shit.*"

Now Clarence felt like he might cry too. Instead, he put an arm around Lucy's shoulders. She leaned against him, her wet hair soaking through his shirt quickly, but he didn't mind.

"You're not a bad kid. You're a good kid, a good friend."

From above them came the paper tearing sound Lucy had heard earlier. She jumped off the couch and saw her mother's ear disappearing into the wall. Lucy couldn't quell her yelp of surprise and fear. Clarence had twisted around to look up with wide eyes and a gaping mouth. Lucy grabbed his hand that was resting on his thigh. He stumbled after her as she pulled him toward the door.

"Let's get out of here!" she said. "You can take us out. I can't get away without you."

"But when I wake up, you'll be lost in the fog

again."

Lucy stopped, one hand on the doorknob. "I know." Her fingers fidgeted with the knob. "If I stay out in the fog, do you promise to find me?"

Clarence felt the hand that held his trembling. "I won't know how to find you."

Her hand fell from the doorknob, her shoulders drooping.

Clarence jumped when he heard the bedroom door open behind them. He took a deep breath, released it, turned to face the hallway.

"Stay behind me."

"Brave Sir Knight!" she said, hands clasped in front of her chest.

The hallway was shadowed, but Clarence could see her silhouetted in the bedroom's doorway. She walked down the hall slowly, unsteadily. As she came into the gray light of the living room, her arms lifted, spread. Her wide smile wasn't in her voice.

"Welcome home."

Clarence shrieked.

His mother stood before him, IV tubes trailing from her arms. The smell of industrial disinfectant filled the air and a machine wailed monotonously. Her face was speckled with blood down to her chin and it was on her teeth, bared in a grin, but her eyes were half-lidded, unfocused.

Clarence disappeared with a sound like a started gasp.

Lucy, exposed now, collapsed to the floor, screaming.

Victoria let her arms fall to her sides. She considered her blubbering daughter, then walked to the window.

The world appeared to her as it always had: gray, lifeless, without form or meaning. When she'd met him, she'd thought Richard could bring her the life she craved, the life she feared. But her husband had been empty as well, and the two of them had drifted together until Lucy had come into their lives, usurping Victoria's body and mangling her emotions. Her daughter had provided no more depth to her life than Richard had, and she began to fear that the world they lived in held nothing for them. She'd tried to save them, the three of them, but had failed.

Lucy's sobs had tapered off into sniffles behind her, and Victoria turned, a small smile lifting the corners of her mouth.

"Do you miss your father?"

Lucy looked up from the carpet, which was damp with her tears. Her mother's smile had vanished and the girl saw the same straight-faced expression her mother always wore, even as she'd lowered her into the bath that one last time. Lucy shuddered and she pulled on her hair, wringing water out.

Finally, she nodded.

"You don't seem very sure about that," Victoria said. "A good girl would have answered yes immediately. All good girls love their fathers."

Lucy shrank down, embarrassed. Then, she asked, "Do you miss Daddy?"

Her mother's face folded into a frown. "No.

Your father left us here. It's his fault the world is gray." She crossed the room to stand over Lucy, who still crouched on the floor. "If he'd come with us, it would be sunny every day, and every day would be summer and the three of us could do whatever we wanted, all the time."

Lucy's eyes brightened, but she scooted away from her mother a little.

"Wouldn't that be nice?" Victoria asked.

Slowly, Lucy nodded. "That's why you look for him? Even if you don't miss him?"

"You're right." Victoria stooped and pinched Lucy's cheek too hard, Lucy squeezing another pair of tears from her eyes. "What a smart little girl you are." She straightened and crossed to the couch, sat. "Yes, I go looking for him so that we can have the life we were meant to have."

Victoria patted next to her. Lucy got up and walked over, sitting on the couch obediently, but leaning away from her mother. With an exasperated sigh, Victoria dragged Lucy onto her lap and held her stiffly. Lucy sat with her back straight, her arms hanging limp, unsure of what to do.

"I found him, your father. He wouldn't come home with me."

"You could make him come home," Lucy said. Her mother's magic was powerful, had controlled the king for so long that Lucy was shocked.

"I could," Victoria mused, her smile surfacing again, making Lucy cringe. "I could, but he got away so quickly and I don't know if I can ever find him again."

They fell silent and Victoria kept her arms around Lucy, but didn't rock her back and forth like Lucy thought mothers should. She started rocking, hoping that her mother would move with her, but she didn't. After a few moments, she stopped and sat still.

"You know what I wish?" Victoria asked. Lucy shook her head. "I wish Clarence was your father." She looked down at her daughter, and it was like looking at a picture of herself when she'd been that age. Her anger flared and she wanted to squeeze Lucy as hard as she could. Instead, she swallowed her desire and asked, "Would you like it if Clarence was your father?"

Again, Lucy hesitated before answering. Clarence had now left her twice, even after promising to protect her, but she couldn't tell her mother that. Still, while he'd been here with her, he was the best friend she'd ever had, her only friend. Even though her daddy had played with her once in a while, he hadn't been as good at it as Clarence. He'd never climbed trees with her, never called her m'lady, never given her candy. Finally, she nodded.

Victoria's lips tightened and she pressed Lucy's head against her chest.

"I'm going to need your help then."

14

Clarence turned the shower off and braced himself against the wall, letting the water drip from his raw, red skin. He was looking down into the drain, still hearing the water plinking into the trap. Even if this drain led to pipes in another apartment, he never would have heard anyone's voice because of the standing water. Shivering, he draped a clean towel around his shoulders.

After he was dry, he dressed. It was 3:18 A.M. and Mike and Val would be over in thirteen hours and forty-two minutes, just enough time to give the apartment a thorough cleaning.

Clarence turned the bathroom light off. In the darkness, he looked into his reading room. Faint light filtered through the venetian blinds, and he could just make out corners of his desk, the soft curve of his recliner.

He closed his eyes and pictured Lucy's bedroom, her bed in the corner where his bookcase was; their desks in almost the same position, except hers was child-size garage sale and his was IKEA. Clarence put his hand out in the darkness and took a step forward. He took another step, another. He should have touched the corner of his desk already. He thought he'd been able to see it in the darkness. He should turn on the light, but didn't want to, was afraid of what he might see.

He reached forward, a little bit at a time, anticipating contact at every moment. When he finally touched the wall, he jumped in surprise, then chuckled a little. He'd gotten himself turned around in the little room. Repositioning himself with the window more directly to his right, he slid his fingers along the wall, their whispering loud in the silence.

Before he could reach the desk, however, his fingers skipped over a small dent in the wall.

He thought he'd damaged the wall wrestling his desk into place the day he'd moved in. Overcome with guilt, he'd called Bob O'Neil.

"In the second bedroom?" Bob had asked, the fluttering sound of a keyboard and a mouse being double-clicked in the background. After a moment, he'd cursed under his breath, then said, "No, you didn't do that. That was from the previous tenants, when their—when they moved out. They were supposed to fix it when the walls were painted, but then you liked the colors and I guess it slipped my mind that this was also on the work order." He'd paused for a deep breath. "I'd be happy to have someone come by with some patch at your earliest convenience. How's this weekend for you?"

The idea of someone being in his apartment with his germs so soon after moving in, before he'd had a chance to sterilize had made Clarence's breath clog in his throat.

"No! That's okay. It's really not that bad and my desk covers it anyway so there's no reason for anyone to go out of their way. Sorry to bother you."

Clarence jerked his fingers away from the wall, lunged toward the light switch near the door. The room burst into light and he looked over his shoulder, turning around in a fast circle, trying to catch sight of anything that might explain why he had felt a small tug on the hem of his shirt.

The light switch clicked. Clarence stopped, his neck craned around. Slowly, he straightened out, walked over to the switch, which clicked again. As he got closer, he saw the switch move down, tremble at the tipping point, the light flickering once, before it snapped back up. After a moment, it moved again, this time breaking the connection, the room going dark.

Clarence stood, his hands clasped in front of his chest, squeezing so that his knuckles strained against the skin. He tried not to breathe as his socked feet pushed into the carpet pile with hardly any sound and he crept from his reading room into the living room.

At a younger age, he might have gone to his bedroom and hidden under the covers. Now, he went to the closet by the front door, opened it as softly as he could, and got a can of Lemon Pledge. The metal canister was cold in his hand, reassuring, and the smell that had dried on its nozzle comforted him.

Clarence put his back against the front door, looking into his dark apartment. He switched the Lemon Pledge from one hand to the other when they'd start to go numb from how hard he was holding the can and he shut his eyes after about fifteen minutes of thinking he saw shadows moving across the thin bars of light that shone through his blinds from the parking lot and he breathed as shallowly and as quietly as possible. Other than that, he didn't move a muscle until the sun started to rise.

Sunday

15

As the sun came up, Clarence allowed his eyes to open, first one, and then the other. There was nothing and no one in his apartment. The shadows he'd seen during the night must've come from outside, and the sounds of running water and crying from some other apartment. He berated himself for wasting so much time being childish.

After he showered, he cleaned the apartment more thoroughly than he had since he'd moved in. He vacuumed and steamed the carpet, scrubbed and Pledged the linoleum. He washed the walls, ceilings and dusted the air vents. He dusted, dusted, dusted. He changed the filters in his air purifiers, even though they weren't due until December, and cranked them up to high. He needed to turn the volume up on the Lions pre-game show on Fox, which scared him a little because the men sitting around the table were yelling at each other and the game hadn't even started yet. He used the hose and attachments of the steam-vac to clean his couch and chair. They were still a little damp, but that wasn't the problem. The dishes had been done, put away, and a cycle to clean the dishwasher started. The trash had been taken out. Sweaty after cleaning, he'd taken another shower. His dirty clothes from yesterday and this morning had been washed along with his sheets and every towel in the apartment, but none of that was the problem.

He just wasn't ready.

He felt it in his stomach, in the back of his throat which bubbled with acid. He tried drinking some water, but it burned on the way down and sloshed around with every movement, making him seasick. His temples pounded with a stress headache.

Clarence paced the apartment, wiping things that had already been cleaned, straightening books on shelves, moving furniture, then nudging it back into place. It was 4:30 and he should have been happy that the apartment was ready, even if he wasn't, but it only made him worry that he'd forgotten something.

Walking past the dining room, he happened to glance up at the light fixture hanging from the ceiling. He'd forgotten to dust and polish it. Fretting, he got out a fresh rag that would need to be washed, stepped on a padded chair that would need to be steamed again, touched the top of the table that would need to be re-sanitized and started dusting the light shade.

Standing on the chair, precariously balanced and holding the light by a slim corner, the enormity of what he'd done, what he'd committed to, rushed in on him and he started coughing. Clarence slapped a hand over his mouth and, his face turning red, then purple, teetered off the chair and rushed to the bathroom.

Clarence got the lid of the toilet up and gagged into the cold, clear water. His stomach muscles clenched, but nothing came out. After the fit had passed, he got up and went to the sink, wet a washcloth with cold water and wiped his face.

"I can't let them come over," he groaned.

"You don't need them."

Clarence didn't look around. "Lucy?"

"You don't need them," she repeated.

"I thought you said that everybody needs friends."

"I'm your friend."

Clarence turned around to face the tub. "Are you okay? Did your mother hurt you again?"

"No!" She paused, then said, "Mommy would never hurt me. She loves me and only wants what's best for me."

"You sound like you've been crying."

She didn't answer, and Clarence waited as long as he dared before looking at his watch. Now, it was quarter to five, and he had too much to do and it was probably too late to call Val and cancel without looking crazy. So he retraced his steps out to the dining room, cleaning as he went, watching the clock, his stomach knotting tighter with each passing minute.

In the parking lot, Mike and Val got out of the car, leaves crunching under their feet as they walked up to Clarence's apartment. Mike held a paper bag with a 6-pack of Bud and a pint of Jim Beam. They hadn't known what to get Clarence and Mike hadn't wanted to call him, insisting that they were going to Clarence's apartment, he probably already had what he wanted to drink. Val had argued, gotten out her cell phone, but then put it away when he'd threatened to just go home.

"Why are you being such a dick?" she'd asked.

He said the same thing standing in front of Clarence's door that he'd said then: "Let's just get this over with."

Clarence was cleaning the underside of the dining table, just in case, when he glanced over his shoulder at the sliding glass door. He saw Mike and Val and sighed, his stomach cinching a little tighter. He was relieved that Mike and Val hadn't blown him off, but was still scared of them being in his apartment. He waved at them through the glass, but they didn't wave back, their eyes focused straight ahead.

He sprinted to his bedroom and tossed the rag inside, shutting the door behind him. Then, he went to the kitchen and popped the top of the waiting bottle of Black Jack Cola. He'd gone to the corner market for chips and dip and spent ten minutes staring at the refrigerator cases, trying to decide on a drink he might like, knowing that he wouldn't have an excuse today. All the beer looked the same, and Mike seemed like the kind of guy to make fun of anyone drinking anything too brightly colored. Clarence knew that Jack Daniels was whiskey, so he thought Mike and Val would both approve.

He heard a murmur from the front door, then a knock, and he upended the bottle and swigged the dark liquid. It smelled sweet, tickling his nose, but then kicked him in the face when he swallowed. Clarence groaned, eyelids fluttering as he shuddered. Smacking his tongue against the roof of his mouth to clear the taste, he poured half the bottle into the sink.

He was just a normal guy, relaxing with some friends on a Sunday afternoon, half his drink already gone by the time they got there. He went to answer the door.

As soon as the door opened, Mike barged into the room, reaching for him. Clarence scuttled away quickly, one hand tightly holding the bottle, the other pressed against his thigh. He made a mental note to wipe the door handle as soon as he could. He turned away, but looked back over his shoulder, both to keep an eye on Mike, but also to be a good host and seem inviting.

"Come on in," he said. "You can put your coats on the dining room chairs."

—and that was okay because he'd thoroughly steamed the one he'd stood on.

Mike frowned, stalking into the room. Val followed more sedately, closing the door behind her.

Clarence took a deep breath of the reassuringly clean air, said over the loud hum of the air purifiers, "Lions look good through their first drive." Another game had been on in the background as he'd cleaned this afternoon. He was pleased at how knowledgeable and natural he sounded. He made a beeline for the chair, leaving them the couch.

The only downside was that they would need to walk past him to get to it.

Val crossed the room to the couch, her eyes on the TV, Clarence watching her out of the corner of his eyes.

"How's Stafford looking?" she asked.

Clarence smiled, relaxed a little. “Two completes, one to Johnson, the other to Best. Best ran for a first down, then got stuffed for a loss of three.” The words felt unfamiliar in his mouth, but he relished it.

Mike forced a smile when Val looked around at him. “I’ll just put the beer in the fridge, huh?”

“Okay,” Clarence said, looking around. “Kitchen’s in there.”

“Yeah, I can see that, thanks.”

“Hey,” Val said, opening the chips that were on the table. “Mix me a Beam and Coke?”

“Yeah, sure, whatever.”

Clarence hoped that the ice had had time to solidify after he’d sanitized the trays this morning, along with everything else in the refrigerator.

“He’s only got Pepsi,” Mike said from the kitchen.

“Whatever,” Val said around a mouthful of chips. “Same thing.”

“Actually,” Clarence said. “They’re not. They list the same basic recipe, but the citric acid in Coca-Cola comes from lemons, and the citric acid in Pepsi comes from oranges.”

Val grunted, then said, “Interesting.”

“Yeah, I read an article about it one time.”

Mike came into the living room, keeping a sharp eye on Clarence as he passed by the chair. His hands were full, but he’d gladly drop his beer if it meant stealing a five and winning.

After leaving the bar last night, he’d taken Val

home and then hinted strongly that maybe he shouldn't be driving. She'd been teasing him all night, pushing her body against his when she'd squeezed past to go up to the bar, even though it wasn't that crowded. He pressed her hard about crashing at her place, but of course she knew what was going on and shut him down.

"I'm sure you're fine," she'd said. "You didn't even drink much and I've seen you way wrecked and not even think about it."

"What if I get pulled over?" He hadn't been able to keep from whining. "My car'll get impounded."

"I'll come bail you out. And I owe you some rides anyway," she'd said, then slammed the door in his face.

So yeah, Mike wanted to get this over with and get what was coming to him.

Clarence leaned away from Mike as he walked past, masking it by reaching for the remote, which sat on the table.

Val saw his open hand and leaned toward him, but then the ceiling thundered overhead, and she jumped. Mike, who was sitting down next to Val, bolted back up, spilling a little of Val's drink onto the coffee table. Startled by their sudden movement, Clarence bobbled the remote.

Noticing the spill, he stood up and said, "Here, let me get that."

"What the hell was that?" Val asked, looking outside. The sky was the cold blue of November in Michigan.

"What the fuck?" Mike echoed.

"Oh," Clarence said, walking quickly to the front closet. "Neighbors upstairs. The older one beats up on the younger one a lot. I barely even hear it anymore."

"Man," Mike said, sipping his beer. "I'm so glad I was an only child."

"Yeah, your parents learned their lesson quick, huh?" Val made the same joke she always made. Then she said to Clarence, "Not me. One brother and three sisters. And I was the youngest." She gulped a third of her drink. "It sucked. You?"

"What?" Clarence asked. He hadn't heard her because the kids upstairs went thundering to another room. He bent over the table from the side opposite Mike and Val to clean the spot of her spilled drink.

"Any brothers or sisters?"

"Oh. No, no brothers or sisters. I had one friend, Mickey. He was—" He shuddered, remembering them pressing their spit-soaked palms together, wondering if Mickey was still alive. "—like a brother. But no, no real brothers. Or sisters."

Clarence cleaned up the spot with one rag, motioned for Mike and Val to move their drinks, sprayed the whole table top with something that stung their noses from an unmarked bottle. After he'd mopped the table with a different rag, he misted the table top with Lemon Pledge, wiping it off with a third rag, all the time feeling the weight of Mike's and Val's eyes on him. His face burned with shame and he glanced at them, but they were stoically watching the game, obviously pretending to not notice. After the table was dry, he put the two bottles back in the closet and took the rags to his bedroom.

While he was gone, Mike nudged Val. He's fucking crazy, he mouthed.

Val ignored him. As Clarence came back in, the kids upstairs stomped back into the living room and Val could've sworn that she saw the ceiling shake.

"Man, how the hell you live with that?"

Clarence shrugged. "I don't even really notice it anymore. Except in the mornings sometimes, when they're getting ready for school—"

"They wake you up?" Mike said.

"No, I'm usually already awake—"

"You get up that early?" Val asked. "Why?"

"I don't know." Clarence shrugged. "I get up when I wake up, and I'm in the shower before I know it. Then, why would I go back to bed, you know?"

"Yeah, I guess."

Mike took a drink and Clarence took one as well. The Black Jack Cola was starting to taste good, sweet, but different. Driving down the field, the Lions started to fizzle. Two run attempts were stopped at the line and a long pass attempt to Calvin Johnson was broken up. Clarence drank when Mike drank, cheered when they cheered, groaned when they groaned.

"Come on!" Mike yelled at the TV.

"Come on," Clarence echoed, smiling.

"That totally should've been pass interference." Val took another big gulp of her drink.

Clarence tried to take as big a gulp, but it fizzed

in his nose and made him gag. Through a superhuman force of will, he only coughed lightly into his hand, then got up to wash his hands. "Totally," he agreed.

When he got up, Mike downed the rest of his beer, then held out the can and said, "Hey Clarence, get me another while you're up?"

Val finished her drink and held out her glass. "Me too."

Clarence stared at them both, mouth hanging open with some excuse locked in his throat.

"You're out, right?" Mike asked. "First one out gets the next round."

Val nodded and Clarence could do nothing but slowly agree and take Val's outstretched glass. He trudged to the kitchen, trying to think of what to do. They'd take their drinks from his diseased hands. His germs would flood into their mouths and they'd probably be sick before the intermission of the game.

Clarence reached the kitchen. No, he could do this. He just needed to take the proper precautions. First, he washed his hands, relishing the warm water and soap between his fingers. While his hands were wet and still fresh, he washed Val's glass, rinsed out Mike's beer can and set them in the dish rack to drip. Grabbing a fresh towel, he dried his hands, then put on a pair of vinyl gloves. He dried Val's glass with another towel and mixed her drink. He had no idea what he was doing, but half Jim Beam, half Pepsi sounded about right. Taking a beer for Mike out of the refrigerator, he set it on the counter next to Val's drink. Then, he sanitized both glass and can with Lysol

Wipes.

Then, Clarence made a decision. He took the gloves off, doused his hands with hand sanitizer and rubbed vigorously. Then, he grabbed the drinks, which slipped a little in his still-moist hands, and hurried out to the living room.

Mike and Val held out their hands for their fresh drinks, but Clarence pretended not to notice and set them down on the coffee table, offering a weak smile when he made a show of noticing their exasperated expressions. Mike opened his beer, which hissed, and Val was about to take a drink, but then stopped, her lower lip touching the glass, her nostrils flaring.

"Whoa!" she said. Taking a small sip, she grimaced. "Geez! What, you trying to get me drunk?"

"I'm sorry," Clarence said. "I've…" He trailed off, then blurted, "I've never mixed a drink before."

Val looked skeptical, but more sympathetic than Mike did. She stood with glass in hand and gestured for Clarence to go ahead of her.

"Come on, I'll show you how to make a drink."

They went into the kitchen, and Clarence realized he was trapped. It was narrow, counters on both sides, only room for one person at a time. By letting him go ahead of her, Val blocked his only way out, and she was moving further into the kitchen, closer to him. Clarence tried to breathe shallowly, but his heart raced, making him dizzy. For a moment, Clarence didn't think that Val would stop, that she'd keep walking until they touched, hugged, kissed, and he couldn't let that happen even though he wanted to but he couldn't think, couldn't move, couldn't do anything. His lower stomach tightened with anticipation and desire; at the same time, he thought he might throw up.

Val didn't seem to have any such thoughts, though. She stopped well within arm's reach, but didn't come any closer. She smiled, looked down, then back up at him from under lowered eyelids. Blinking slowly, her smile sweetened.

"Glasses?" she asked, her voice low and husky.

"Oh—uh…" He pointed at the cupboard above the sink.

Val got out a juice glass, poured about a finger's width of Jim Beam. The amber liquid sparkled under the compact fluorescent bulb. She held up the glass so Clarence could see the liquor's level, and he nodded. Then, she filled the glass halfway with Pepsi and swirled the mixture. The liquor lightened the almost-black cola, making it a deep, rich brown. Val put the glass to her nose, resting her lower lip against the rim. She inhaled, smiling still, and her eyes closed when she tilted the glass, puckered her lips to drink.

Clarence couldn't help leaning forward, moaning softly.

"Hey!" Mike said as he rounded the corner. "How long does it take to make a frigging drink?"

Clarence jumped. "Oh! Val was, uh… showing me how—" Then, he stopped, because Mike knew what he and Val were supposed to be doing. He pressed his hands against his upper thighs, realizing that now they both had him trapped, and he was barely breathing now, his vision graying around the edges.

Val didn't seem bothered, and said, "Did we miss anything important?"

"Yeah," Mike said. "Lions punted."

"That's not really exciting." Val pouted. She turned back to Clarence, and said, "Thanks for the..." She paused, and Clarence smiled when she did. "For the drink," she finished.

Clarence watched her brush past Mike, who still stared at him. Growing uncomfortable, Clarence opened the refrigerator so he stood behind the door, reached over to get another Black Jack. Mike came no closer, didn't go back to the living room, just stood there.

"You go ahead," Clarence said, setting the bottle on the counter. "I need to wash my hands."

Mike turned away slowly, and Clarence ostentatiously washed his hands.

Val was having a hard time not laughing. She was going to win and she knew exactly how she was going to do it. Clarence obviously didn't know anything about drinking, and now he was confused as well. As an added bonus, she was making sure that Mike earned what he was going to get from her. She wouldn't be the one on the short end of a stick in a relationship ever again.

Mike sat back down. He wasn't cheering or groaning at the game anymore, just drinking. Clarence still copied him, but cheered when Val cheered, spilling his drink onto himself. He excused himself, wobbled when he stood up and disappeared back to the bedroom.

Clarence came back with different pants on, and now Val did laugh, which made Clarence blush, but she didn't call him weird, so he smiled, and took another drink, tilting the bottle up, up, up.

He lowered it and was about to push himself out of the chair again, when Val slammed her drink and stood, seemingly in one motion.

"I'm out, who wants one?"

"Me, please," Clarence said in a sing-song voice, realizing that he was drunk, this was what being drunk was like, and he snickered without knowing what was so funny.

Clarence felt immensely grateful that he didn't need to stand up, but he wasn't so drunk that he was completely careless. He held onto his empty bottle, tilting it up again and pretending that he was still drinking the last little bit.

It was half-time, not intermission, and Val went to the kitchen to get the next round. Mike craned his neck toward the clinking sounds, then scooted across the couch closer to Clarence. Clarence's heart skipped a beat and his hand clenched around the bottle and on his thigh, tracing the hard plastic of the bottle of hand sanitizer in his pocket.

Mike leaned closer and said, "Hey man, I just wanted to say, I see the way you look at Val, and I gotta tell you, I don't like it." His lips pulled back, baring his teeth for a moment. "Whatever you're thinking, I don't like it."

Clarence didn't know what to say, his brain a jumble of half-remembered dreams, wishful thinking and what he thought had happened in the kitchen. It seemed to be a good thing that he couldn't think of anything to say, because Mike nodded, still frowning, and sat back as Val bustled into the room, balancing three drinks.

Val pretended not to notice the change in seating arrangement, again struggling to keep a straight face. This would be even more perfect. She walked to her seat next to Mike and set the drinks on the coffee table. She set Mike's beer in front of him and he grunted thanks. Then, she picked up the bottle of Black Jack and leaned over to hand it to Clarence.

It was going to happen right in front of him, Mike realized too late. Clarence reached for the bottle and his open hand was right there, but all Mike could do was groan at the thought of how long she'd gloat about this.

Val stopped leaning forward, pretending that she was at her limit, and Clarence stretched that much further. His eyes focused as if he realized what he was doing and he tried to snatch his hand away, but it was too late. Val's other hand shot forward and she stole a five from Clarence, the sound of their palms slapping loud and sharp.

Val started laughing, pumping her fists in the air and raising the roof. Mike would be buying her drinks forever.

Mike groaned, but was smiling too. At least it was over now. He'd struggle through whatever Val wanted him to do, and maybe he'd even enjoy it. He hoped that she would at least stop teasing him now.

Clarence stood aghast, staring at his reddened palm.

"Val," he said, his voice weak. "You need to wash your hands."

Val couldn't hear him over her own laughter. "What?"

Clarence looked up at her, tears in his eyes. "You need to wash your hands."

"What, why?" She looked at Mike and giggled when he shook his head.

Clarence blushed, thinking that now she was laughing at him. "You'll get sick. I don't want you to get sick." He stood. "You need to wash your hands now."

"Don't be stupid," she said. "I'm not going to get sick."

"Please, just go wash your hands," he whined, then began digging in his pocket. "I have—sanitizer…"

Mike was laughing at him now and Clarence turned a darker shade of red and his vision narrowed. He saw only Val, her hand that was now crawling with his germs hanging by her side. Soon, his germs would multiply and spread up her arm, reach her mouth, her eyes, her nose, get on anything she touched, make her sick, make Mike sick, make everyone in the world sick. He stepped over Mike, careful not to touch him or her, even though he was close enough to feel her breath on his face.

"Here. Please. Sanitizer."

The intensity in his voice unnerved her and she stepped away from him. She laughed, but stopped when her voice trembled. "It's okay, really."

"Please," he said, holding out the hand sanitizer. "Just let me—"

"Oh, for god's sake." She licked the palm of her hand, then held it up, the light flashing on her saliva. "See? I told you, I'm—"

Clarence's red face darkened to almost purple, his mouth hung open like he was screaming, but was mute. The hand that held the sanitizer trembled. Every other inch of his body seemed frozen.

Val moved around the coffee table, jumping when Mike slapped his leg, laughing at Clarence's expression. Val relaxed a little, smiling.

Clarence lunged at Val.

She stumbled back, slamming into the entertainment center. Clarence tripped over the coffee table and knocked her legs out from underneath her, and she fell on top of him. Val tried to crawl off of him and away, but he caught her hand and pulled her back, pouring hand sanitizer into it. She almost slipped free, but Clarence clamped down on her wrist so hard she couldn't move her fingers.

Val flashed back to her last boyfriend, who used to tie her up to fuck her, and she froze. She should just let Clarence do what he wanted. It would be over soon, and struggling would just make it worse.

But that was bullshit, and she tried to shake loose again.

Then, Clarence started reaching for her face, pulling her down and closer to him. Val panicked and tried to jerk her arm free, but he was too strong. He used that one distracted second to wrench her arm, forcing her to the floor. He crawled on top of her and slapped her hands away as she reached up to try and push him off.

Mike stopped laughing. Something was wrong. His mind felt a little fuzzy, but Clarence wasn't just being strange. Val was screaming and he had to do something. This was his chance.

"Hey!" he snapped, his voice deeper than normal. He jumped forward and grabbed Clarence's wrist, intending to pull him off, maybe hit him, mostly because he wanted payback for the headache that he'd been the last few days.

Clarence spun around, moved with Mike trying to pull him away, and Mike lost his balance. Then, Clarence shoved him, and Mike's shirt was drenched, clinging to him and smelling like alcohol. He fell backward over the coffee table and hit his head on the arm of the couch, padded, but hard underneath, which stunned him.

Val felt Clarence's weight leave and tried to push herself up, but then Clarence was back on top of her and now his knees were on her chest and she couldn't move, couldn't breathe and she started to panic.

Clarence had sanitized her hand, but she'd licked her palm. His germs were in her mouth and it was probably too late, but hopefully not. He clamped his knees on either side of her head to hold her still, then poured hand sanitizer into her mouth.

Val sputtered, trying to spit it out, letting more in. She gagged.

Mike struggled to his feet, swayed for a moment, heard Val, thought Clarence was choking her, and dove at him.

Clarence didn't know what to do now. He'd gotten some sanitizer into Val's mouth, but not nearly enough, and now he was out, and he'd touched her all over. She needed a shower. He was shifting his weight to stand and drag her to the bathroom when Mike tackled him.

Mike landed on top of Clarence and started hitting him. The first punch landed on his shoulder; the next, the left side of Clarence's face. Val rolled away, and Mike swung harder, showing off.

Val touched his shoulder and he stopped punching Clarence and stood up. Then, he saw the tears on Val's face and kicked Clarence in the ribs.

The air left Clarence's lungs and he clutched his side, struggling to breathe.

"What the fuck, asshole?" Mike said, his voice hoarse, realizing he'd been screaming at Clarence the whole time. Mike started to kneel down for round two.

Val stopped him. "Please. Let's just go."

Mike kicked him one last time and stomped to the door. He opened it, then stood there, waiting for Val. "Come on, let's go."

She was looking down at Clarence, tears running down her face.

Still struggling for breath, Clarence managed to say, “Make him—wash his hands.”

Clarence coughed, seeming to breathe out forever, his vision graying. One moment, Val was standing over him, the next she was gone, and the door slammed. He tried to rise, to rush after them, apologize, beg them to not think he was a freak, tell them they should take hot showers as soon as they could, but he was losing consciousness. The left side of his face felt bigger than it should, and the right hurt only a little less. Mike had punched him in the throat, and what little breath he drew burned.

He blinked slowly, his muscles relaxing as they gave up the fight against unconsciousness and he thought he saw someone standing over him. Her black hair hid her face, her fingers cool on his face. She smoothed his hair back, took off his glasses, one lens now cracked.

“Lucy?”

She shushed him, and he thought she smiled, though her voice hissed. “She deserved it.”

Monday

16

Clarence groaned, stirred. Opening his mouth for air hurt. His lungs pushed against sore ribs. His face felt hot, but numb at the same time. He reached up and gasped at the way the bones in his broken nose grated against each other. He nearly passed out again and could only pant while the ceiling above him came back into focus.

It felt like a long time before he was able to sit up, which he did slowly. Something shifted in his face, and blood poured out of his nose and down the front of his shirt. At the same time, his stomach cramped and he stumbled and crawled to the bathroom, barely making it in time to lift the toilet lid and vomit the blood he'd swallowed while unconscious. He almost lost consciousness again, but couldn't quite make it. It would have been a welcome reprieve from stomach muscles that had joined his body's chorus of pain.

The porcelain was cool against his hot and swollen skin, and he moved only when the spot where his head lay became too warm. He reached up and flushed the toilet, the rushing water making a slight breeze that also felt good, but as he returned to fuller awareness, he realized what a mess he was.

Unable to stand, he wormed out of his clothes.

He flopped over to the tub, turning on the shower and hauling himself over the side to lie on the floor. The water was as cold as a blessing, then turned hot as he cranked the handle. The steaming water scalded even worse than usual, washing the blood from his inflamed face. Clarence began to cry, desperately trying not to let his face constrict, which made it hurt more.

There came a soft squeak and the steaming water cooled to comfortingly warm. Clarence didn't open his eyes, didn't want to see the hand he visualized withdrawing to the other side of the curtain; and if he saw it going down the drain—

This surprised a disbelieving laugh out of him, which turned to sobs, which tapered off.

"Thank you," he whispered, mouth barely moving.

There was no answer, but he knew she was there.

Clarence sat up, still not trusting his legs. He couldn't reach his shampoo or body wash, but could reach the clean washcloth. Wiping tenderly at his face, especially around his nose, bits of dried blood flaked off and ran down the drain. Rising up on his knees, he got his soaps and washed. The water turning cold from use, it no longer felt good and he shivered, turning off the shower and groping along the wall for the clean towel hanging there.

Hesitating, he pushed the curtain back, but there was no little girl in the bathroom. Clarence sighed in relief and, after drying off, started cleaning the bathroom.

He worked his way back out to the living room, following the trail of red drops on the carpet and scrubbing them with ammonia and cold water. He reached where he'd lain in the living room, the floor still vaguely warm and a puddle of blood in a V-shape where it had spilled between his legs when he sat up. He blotted up as much as he could, then poured half of the watered-down ammonia directly onto the stain, giving it a moment to work its way in.

The TV was still on, so he turned it off. Mike's can was still on the coffee table, but his bottle and Val's glass were on the floor next to the empty hand sanitizer. Clarence's numb and swollen lips couldn't quiver, but he felt tears welling up again. Pushing himself up, he staggered to his phone, which sat on the table next to the chair he'd sat in yesterday and began scrolling backward through the Caller I.D.

Her number wasn't hard to recognize. It was the only one with a local area code. It rang once, then went to voicemail.

"Val, it's Clarence." His voice sounded strange to him, and he tried to clear his throat. "I'm sorry about that. I just wanted to say sorry for yesterday. I don't know what got into me—"

Except he did know, but he pushed what he knew out of his mind.

Now it was hard to talk, so he choked out, "I'm sorry. I can't tell you how sorry. Just—just don't think I'm weird." He paused, drew a shuddering breath. "See you later."

Clarence put the phone down, went back to the

bloodstain and knelt on the carpet.

"You know, don't you?"

He kept scrubbing, not wanting to look around.

"You know, so just say it."

"No," Clarence said, mostly to himself, unsure whether the voice was coming from the hallway leading to the bathroom or his own mind. "It was just a mistake. Go back to your drain."

"They hate you now."

"No! It was a mistake. You'll see. I'll see them, apologize, explain. They'll understand. They're my friends."

"I'm your friend."

"Yes." He stopped scrubbing. "But they're my friends too. You're not my only friend."

"No. Mother is your friend too. She likes you."

"What?" Clarence twisted around quickly, which made him dizzy and nauseous again and he almost fell over. The room behind him was empty. "I thought you didn't like your mom."

"It was just a mistake." Her voice came from over his shoulder, out of sight again.

Clarence thought she was smiling as she said it, and he bent back down to keep scrubbing.

Mike had been grinning, Clarence remembered now. His lips had stretched from ear to ear and his teeth had looked huge as he'd hit Clarence. Val hadn't looked sorry for him as she'd stood over him, after Mike had left. She'd said something, but he couldn't grasp it. He'd already started to lose consciousness.

"She said, "I'm sorry,"" he reassured himself.

"They don't hate me."

Clarence felt a little better now that the stain was coming out and also because Lucy didn't say anything further. Eventually, satisfied that the stain was gone, he eased up to his feet, stiff and sore from staying in one position for so long. Having a clean apartment would put his mind at ease, and he went to his front closet to get everything.

Pulling out his vacuum, his steamer, his spray bottles and paper towel, he found a box of latex gloves. If only he'd been wearing some yesterday, none of this would have happened.

He couldn't though. He'd tried that before, and with nowhere to go, his germs would turn on him and devour him.

He didn't have a choice. It was bad enough that another person would probably get sick and might even die because of his selfish negligence. He couldn't take the chance of infecting anyone else, ever again. They were his germs. The consequences would also be his.

Clarence pulled a pair of gloves from the box and put them on.

Maybe he shouldn't even go to work today. Or ever. Maybe he should just quit. It was kind of stupid, when he stopped to think about it. He didn't want to make anyone sick, so he spent all day touching people's things, telling himself that he was protecting them, when really, they'd be just as well off if he wasn't there in the first place.

Except, that wasn't true. Now that he was

working with Mike and Val to clean the entire building, he had a chance to make up for their ineffectual work attitude.

Clarence made a difference. He just needed to take appropriate precautions. He put the gloves on, the rubber bands snapping against his wrists. He knew what he needed to do now. When he had been fourteen, he'd worn his yellow Rubbermaid gloves for over a week straight. He'd learned from articles online that his germs continued to grow and multiply and infest under the gloves, so he needed to wash his hands every hour, putting on fresh gloves afterward.

The dent in the wall, in her bedroom, in his office.

She was in his apartment.

"Where are you?" Clarence put down the Lysol spray bottle and roll of paper towels and walked through the apartment. All of the rooms were empty. "Lucy?"

"You hate me now."

She didn't sound sad, like Clarence might have expected. She sounded angry.

"I don't hate you. It's—I'm just trying to figure some stuff out."

Clarence was in his bedroom, and he followed her voice back to the living room. Of course, she wasn't there.

"Mother found him," she said, her voice coming from around the corner, in the kitchen.

"Who?"

"Father."

"That's great!" Clarence followed the voice, but the kitchen was empty.

"No," she said, from the living room again. "It's not."

There was a stretch of silence. Clarence asked her why in his mind, to see if maybe she could hear his thoughts. She didn't reply, and she didn't continue unprompted, which could have maybe given him the illusion that he was imagining this.

"Why? I thought you missed your dad."

"I don't!"

Clarence jumped, startled.

"I mean, I do. All good girls love their fathers. But he didn't want to come home with mother when she found him."

"Oh." It was a lame response, but Clarence couldn't think of anything else to say.

Another few moments passed in silence and he began to feel awkward just standing there. He went to the table where the spray bottle and paper towels were, got up on a chair and began wiping down the light fixture.

"You don't care."

Clarence sighed. "Of course I care. We can talk while I clean, right?"

He fought back the urge to apologize, but he couldn't stand here talking to the air while his germs spread and multiplied around him. He moved on to the sconce on the wall by the front door, then the lamps on either end of the couch.

"You'd make a good father."

Clarence froze, a lamp in one hand and a damp paper towel in the other. He'd never thought about being a father before, because he knew he wouldn't have children. He knew about sex, had even snuck one of his dad's *Penthouses* when he'd been fifteen. The thought of being that close to someone, touching them, sharing each other's germs—it made him nauseous. So whether or not he'd be a good dad had never even entered his mind.

"Why?"

"You're caring," she said, and now her voice was in the hallway, moving toward his bedroom. "You have your priorities, but you still make time for me. I like you."

Clarence followed the voice, but then stopped. "Lucy?"

"I wish you were my father."

"But, your dad—"

"No!"

Clarence shrank away, feeling the force of her personality rushing down the hallway, almost pushing him back. He put his hands over his ears, his swollen face stinging as he stumbled back into the living room.

"It's his fault the world is gray! He wouldn't come with us!"

Clarence fell to his knees when he tried to change direction. She was in front of him now. He could almost see her through his squinted eyes, taller in her anger.

"Even when he got another chance, he wouldn't come!"

Clarence tried to escape, but she was everywhere.

"This isn't how it was supposed to be."

He knocked over a dining room chair sprinting around the corner from the kitchen.

"His fault!"

He slammed his office door behind him, trying to trap her inside, but she was in the living room.

"You can save us!"

His ears hurt, and his head ached, and he worried that people were pounding on walls, the neighbors upstairs stomping on the floor, trying to get him to quiet down. He felt her in the room behind him, the hallway, closing in on him, faster, but then he was in his bedroom and the door was closed with him leaning up against it, bracing for impact.

"We need you," she said, over his shoulder, in his ear.

Clarence yelped and darted out of the room, closing that door and dodging into the bathroom.

His hands on the door, he panted, heart pounding. He was tense, expecting any moment to hear her screaming at him, for the chase to continue. He pressed his palms flat against the door, putting his weight against it. The expected impact, or words at his shoulder, never came.

By degrees, he eased back, still tensed to leap forward again if need be. There was no sound, except for the creak of the ceiling above him, the soft sudden sound of water moving through the pipes in the walls.

Clarence turned away from the door, toward

the shower. Yes, he had something, because he heard it again. The same gurgle from the shower drain he'd heard five days ago. Darting glances back at the door, he leaned over the tub, his face close to the drain. He didn't say anything, afraid to restart the cacophony.

The first whisper was indecipherable.

Clarence couldn't help it. "Lucy?" he whispered. "What's going on?"

He thought he heard her words bubble up the drain, but that was only his mind playing tricks, because that's what he imagined a voice coming out of a shower drain should sound like. He had heard her the first time. He just needed to hear her say it again. His stomach clenched even tighter the second time.

"She's trying," she murmured, "to trick you."

17

Mr. Caruthers didn't know what, but something was wrong with his office. He stood in the doorway, his coat draped over his arm and his lunchbox in one hand, eyes darting here and there. He couldn't find what exactly was wrong, but the drop in his stomach told him that it was because everything was wrong.

"Hey, Jim!" Will Fredericks, the daytime building manager, said from behind him.

Mr. Caruthers turned. Fredericks was fifteen years younger than he was, and a son of a bitch.

"Will."

Mr. Fredericks—Will; Mr. Caruthers couldn't think of him as mister—pushed by him and stood by the desk, one hand resting on the blotter. The desk! That was it! There was something wrong with the desk.

Not just the desk, though.

"Having some trouble with your crew?" Will asked.

"What? No—why? Who told you that?" Mr. Caruthers stomped into the office, pushed past Will to hang his coat in the closet. He did it quickly, not liking the threatening maw hanging open while he was talking with this prick.

Will Fredericks was in charge of maintenance and security, the services that were required during the daytime hours of operation. The building only had one security guard, and Will did most of the maintenance himself. Anything too big for him to handle was contracted out, and that's the way the building owner liked it: keeping as few people on the payroll as possible.

Mr. Caruthers, on the other hand, had three employees working for him.

"Well, you did put another of your guys on probation," Will said. "The 'good' one, right?" He smiled in that slimy way he had. "You know, if you ever need any help managing your people—"

"No!" Mr. Caruthers snapped, feeling his heart pound all the way down his left arm. "I can handle my people. You just keep moving."

Will held his hands up, smirking. "No need to get so defensive. Just thought I'd offer my—"

"I don't need your help."

"Alright, alright," Will said. "Have a nice evening."

Will took his coat from the back of the desk chair. That must've been it: Will's coat hanging on the back of the chair when he was usually gone by the time Mr. Caruthers got there. Except the dislocated feeling of something being different persisted. Will was walking out of the office and Mr. Caruthers was just about to heave a sigh of relief when he turned back.

"Thanks for cleaning the office, by the way. It's nice to know that you do more than walk up and down stairs and harass your janitors all night."

He was gone before Mr. Caruthers could think

of a retort.

That son of a bitch had been keeping tabs on him. What did he do, sit and watch the security tapes from the previous night every day, just to see what Mr. Caruthers did? He was doing his goddamned job, that's what he 'did.'

Mr. Caruthers couldn't stay in the office. He needed to move around. Now was as good a time as any to do his usual walk up to the sixth floor. Clarence, Mike and Val knew their jobs. They could start cleaning without needing to check in with him.

They could do it without him.

The heavy stairwell door boomed shut behind him. Mr. Caruthers put a hand on the banister and started climbing.

Without him.

Four years ago, he'd been pushing hard to be promoted to daytime manager when the old one had retired. The building owner had hired an outside candidate instead and, within months, had cut Mr. Caruthers back to 'technically part-time'. Now, it seemed like Fredericks was running a smear campaign and the painful truth was that, on camera, it probably didn't look like Mr. Caruthers did much of anything.

He paused to rest between four and five, but not because he was out of breath. He was huffing and puffing only slightly.

Reaching the roof door, he checked his watch. Even with the minute of rest, he still matched his average time. Smiling, he turned and began his descent.

He did plenty, plenty that probably didn't show up on tape. Managing the building's supplies, managing three employees. It was easy for Fredericks to say that he did all the maintenance himself, but that meant that ninety percent of the time, he was sitting around, waiting for something to break. Managing security was also a do-nothing job. Walt Crain, the security guard, amounted to a receptionist for the building.

By the time he'd made it back down to the basement, Mr. Caruthers felt better about himself and his job.

Mike and Val were waiting for him in the office.

Val wouldn't look at him, and he wasn't sure, but Mr. Caruthers thought that he saw a dark bruise under the dark skin of her cheek. Mike, on the other hand, was intensely focused on Mr. Caruthers as soon as he came into their field of view. It unnerved him.

"Something you need from me?" he asked, making no move to trap himself inside the tiny office.

"We want you to fire Clarence," Mike said with no hesitation.

"Is that so? Why?"

"We're not working with him anymore. It's us or him."

"Well, it would be a great tragedy to lose you two, but I still haven't heard a reason why I should fire him." Mr. Caruthers paused while Mike's certainty wavered. "You're getting the whole building cleaned on time and he's keeping the two of you off my nerves for the most part. That's win-win for me."

"No, it's not," Mike said. He stopped and turned, but Val wouldn't look at him, so he continued. "We were playing that game on Saturday, and you yelled at us, mostly him. Then, he said we should mess with you, and he showed us how to avoid the cameras, so we did. We listened for you in the stairwell and every time we heard you coming, we acted like nothing was going on."

"Really."

"Yeah. Then, Clarence said we should really mess with your head and clean your office because he said that you'd think something was wrong even though everything was where you'd left it."

Mr. Caruthers's lips tightened. The blood started pounding in his temples, but he kept his voice even. "Anything else?"

Mike blinked, then opened his mouth. After a moment, he said, "He's late again today too."

Mr. Caruthers nodded. "Fine. You don't need to work with him anymore. Two floors apiece and I don't care if you two work to—"

"That's not good enough."

Val barely spoke, but she was loud and clear to Mr. Caruthers. Mike too, who put a comforting hand on her shoulder.

Mr. Caruthers folded his arms and rested them on his stomach. "What happened?"

"Him or us," she said.

"Duly noted. Get to work. You have a building to clean."

Val nodded and walked past him to the elevator. Mike started to say something, then understanding lit his eyes. He nodded and hurried to catch up to Val before the elevator door could close. Mr. Caruthers went into the office and sat at his desk.

Clarence.

A good janitor, but a bad employee. For the last eight years, Mr. Caruthers had let the first part compensate for the second. He'd received many emails complimenting the janitor who worked on 5 and 6 over the years, which astounded him. People never complimented janitors. Most hardly even noticed them. A janitor was only noticed when he didn't do his job.

Like Mike and Val. No matter how many compliments came in about Clarence, four times as many complaints came in about Mike and Val. Not that it was necessarily because they were horrible at their jobs, even though they drove him just as crazy as Clarence did. Most complaints that came in were blown out of proportion and were due to simple mistakes that could happen to anyone.

Except Clarence didn't make mistakes.

Mr. Caruthers leaned back in his chair, which squeaked shrilly beneath him.

"Mr. Caruthers?" a quiet voice said from the doorway.

His heart leaped in his chest and he sat bolt upright and swiveled around sharply. Mr. Caruthers bolted to his feet. "Clarence! What the—"

Clarence's face was swollen, a rainbow of bruises. Val had had a bruise on her cheek. Mike had been keyed up. Mr. Caruthers wondered briefly what had happened, but was thankful it wasn't his problem.

Recovering his poise, he said, "You're late."

"Yes, sir."

They stood, facing each other for a few moments in awkward silence until Mr. Caruthers finally said, "Well?"

Clarence didn't want to tell him what had happened that morning, or that he'd been late on purpose to try to avoid Val, so even though it hurt him to lie to Mr. Caruthers, he said, "There was a traffic jam on M-10."

"That's not my problem," Mr. Caruthers snapped.

Clarence hung his head, his hands tightening on his thighs, and he was wearing latex gloves. His whole posture reminded Mr. Caruthers of a kicked dog, infuriating him. All at once, his decision was made.

"Clarence. You're fired."

Clarence's head snapped up, and the sudden movement sent tears sliding down his cheeks. "No, sir. Please—!"

"This isn't a discussion." Mr. Caruthers sat and got out a termination form. "Mike and Val told me that you were the mastermind behind your little games on Saturday." The scratching of his pen on the triplicate paper was loud in the silence between his words. "You also trespassed, again. Your termination is immed—"

"They told you?"

She'd been right, Clarence thought, still in shock.

Mr. Caruthers stopped writing and turned. Clarence's face was stark white. His lower lip and gloved hands trembled. His entire body seemed to shake and he wasn't blinking. Mr. Caruthers nodded.

"Please, sir," Clarence said. "This is all just a misunderstanding. We—they came over yesterday, and I—we all were drinking and Val—I mean, I—"

Mr. Caruthers held up his hand, and Clarence relaxed ever so slightly.

"You're not being fired for what you did outside of work," he said. "You were warned repeatedly about trespassing after hours, put on probation. You didn't listen." Mr. Caruthers swiveled back to the form on his desk and slashed his signature onto the paper, hating that he'd explained himself over and over to Clarence when he shouldn't need to. "So, you're fired." He tore out the yellow copy.

Clarence looked at the sheet of paper unbelievingly. He remembered when he first interviewed for his job. Mr. Caruthers had sat where was sitting now and asked him why he wanted to be a janitor.

"Because sixty-seven percent of all people who get sick contract the illness while at work," he'd said, which had made Mr. Caruthers blink in surprise. "I don't want anyone to get sick."

Mr. Caruthers had never heard an answer like that, and had hired him on the spot, offering his hand in congratulations.

Clarence had simply stood up, hands and elbows held close to his body. "Thank you," he'd said.

"I won't let you down."

Now, he had.

Clarence couldn't take the termination form. Not while Mr. Caruthers held it. There could be a pinhole in the latex gloves and Clarence's germs would get through and Mr. Caruthers might get sick. It was almost certain that Val was sick right now, and it would spread to Mike, and then to Mr. Caruthers, and Clarence wanted it to happen. He wanted to rip off the gloves, grab Mr. Caruthers's hand, cough on him, spit his germs directly into his mouth and eyes and watch him collapse, shake with fever and gasp for air, just like his mother.

Mr. Caruthers slid his chair back. Clarence's face had gone from white to bright red, his eyes widening, and he'd leaned over at the waist. Tears still leaked from the corners of his eyes, but a grin had spread across his face. He raised his hands, one reaching for the rubber-banded end on his wrist, teeth clacking together as he chewed the air.

Clarence was between him and the door, and he'd already scooted backward. Mr. Caruthers' back was practically against the closet door and his heart hammered while a cold sweat broke out on his forehead. His breathing quick and shallow, Mr. Caruthers shot up out of his chair.

Startled, Clarence realized what he'd been about to do, and instead of reaching forward to touch Mr. Caruthers, he clasped his hands together.

"Please sir! They'll all get sick without me!"

Mr. Caruthers wasn't listening. He stomped

forward, his only thought to escape the small and shrinking office. Clarence scuttled away to avoid being touched, stumbling backward through the office door. Mr. Caruthers breathed a little easier out in the basement, but was furious now.

"Get out! You're fired! Let's go!"

Mr. Caruthers herded Clarence toward the stairwell door, up the stairs and to the front door, not letting him get a word out.

Clarence tried to protest, hiccupping through his tears that he needed to clean the door handle, the banister, the lobby door handle, the main door. Once outside, the enormity of what had happened cascaded in on him and he collapsed to the concrete, sobbing uncontrollably.

Mr. Caruthers looked down on him without pity. "You have one minute to get into your car and drive away, or I'm calling the police."

Clarence stood, wavered on his feet and then stumbled to his car. The building's door shut behind him with a pneumatic whoosh and a soft slam of finality. He got into his car, getting the key in the ignition on the fourth try. Dropping it into gear, he floored it and the car's tires squealed as he cut off a sedan on the service drive. He cut off another car he didn't see through his tears getting onto the freeway and started driving home by instinct.

Clarence shifted in his seat, uncomfortable, and pulled his work keys out from under him. Mr. Caruthers had forgotten to ask for them.

She deserved it, Lucy had said about Val, and

she'd been right.

Mr. Caruthers deserved it too.

Exiting the freeway, Clarence felt calmer now.

Back at the Haimes Building, Clarence went in through the service entrance, hugged the wall to avoid the camera, and crept to the stairwell. He put his ear against the door, listened hard, thought he didn't hear anything, and waited another minute, just to be sure. Then, he pushed the door open as quietly as he could. Above him, he could hear Mr. Caruthers's heavy breathing and the metal-sliding sound of his ring dragging along the banister. Clarence froze. After a few moments, he concluded that Mr. Caruthers was passing either the second or third floor, and going up. Still, Clarence didn't move a muscle or make a sound until he heard a door open and close far above him. Then, he softly shut the door behind him and headed down the stairs to the basement.

Mr. Caruthers exited the stairwell on the fifth floor. Finding Mike and Val in the fourth office down, he couldn't help but smile, even if he was a little concerned at the drastic change. They were all business, Mike moving furniture and dusting, Val running the vacuum. Their faces were blank, lost in thought. Val noticed him standing in the doorway and turned off the vacuum, which made Mike look around.

"I just wanted to let you know," Mr. Caruthers said. "Clarence has been let go. Until a replacement can be found, you two will be responsible for cleaning the entire building." They nodded, and even though he didn't think he needed to, he added, "So step it up."

He waited another moment to see if they needed louder motivation, but Val started vacuuming again, and Mike moved a chair back against the wall, so Mr. Caruthers moved on.

Back in the stairwell, he realized he felt pretty good about what had happened. He decided he wouldn't post the job until it became absolutely necessary. That way, he'd be able to claim that he'd trimmed the fat from his employee budget and show up Fredericks. Mike and Val also seemed to be cowed in some way that he didn't understand, but was grateful for nonetheless. Everything seemed to be going his way, and by the time he opened the door to the basement, he was whistling.

It was ten minutes after six, and as good a time as any to eat dinner. Walking to the office, he paused just inside the door, feeling déjà vu jitter up his spine. Except now he knew what was wrong: the closet door was open.

Mr. Caruthers rolled his eyes. The door was hung slightly crooked in its frame and had a tendency to swing open if not shut all the way. Now, it seemed that the latch was broken, because he knew that he shut it after hanging up his coat. Even that gave him a thrill of satisfaction. He'd put in the work order for Fredericks to fix it and bug him about it every day until it got done.

He moved past the desk chair, which rattled across the concrete, to push the door closed. Then, he was thrown forward, shoved into the closet. The door slammed shut behind him.

Mr. Caruthers bolted up and whirled until he felt dizzy and nauseous, lost his balance. Lying on his side on the floor, he saw the light from behind him, and groped in the dark to find the doorknob. It wouldn't turn. He shook it, then the knob came off in his hand. Trying to force his mind to think rationally and his throbbing left arm to cooperate, he tweezed the post that went through the door and connected the knobs. He would thread the knob back onto the post and get out of here, so there was no need to—

The post was pulled out from between his fingers.

He wanted to shout, but was surprised at how small his voice sounded in the cramped, shrinking space. "Hey?"

He slapped at the door, trying to knock it down, but the contracting closet was squeezing the air out and he couldn't breathe and now the left side of his neck and face was throbbing in time with his racing heart. Mr. Caruthers backed up to take a running start, but bumped into the shelves in the back sooner than he thought and lost his balance. White fireworks exploded across the left half of his vision and as he felt the walls and ceiling close in around him, he lost consciousness.

Clarence stood in front of the door, guilt and regret knotting his stomach. The faint slaps against the door stopped. He heard a clatter, then a low, unidentifiable sound. Then, nothing.

He wanted to open the door, apologize, tell Mr. Caruthers that he'd touched as many surfaces in the closet as he could before he heard the stairwell door open and that Mr. Caruthers should go to the doctor because he was going to get sick.

He also wanted to go home, tell Lucy what he'd done and for her to tell him it was okay, that Mr. Caruthers had deserved it.

Clarence nodded, smiling, and turned away.

18

Clarence's heart was still pounding when he got home. He went straight to the bathroom and leaned close to the drain.

"Lucy, guess what."

There was no answer.

Clarence sat back. He called her name again. Nothing. Getting up, he went room to room, calling for her, but Lucy didn't answer.

He stood in his living room, pondering this for a few moments. The last thing she'd said to him was that she was trying to trick him. Then, nothing. He'd called her name, into the shower drain, the bathroom sink, the one in the kitchen, every room of the house. Then, he'd realized it was time to go to work, and had bustled out the door.

Lucy had acted crazy this morning, chasing him around the apartment and yelling at him. Then, she'd said that she was trying to trick him. So, it must have been a game that she was playing. He would have to tell her that he didn't like it.

Lucy had acted crazy, then said she was trying to trick him.

She was trying to trick him.

Lucy had said that it had been a mistake, that she liked her mother after all. They must have talked, sorted it out, made up. Which was great. Clarence had felt distant from his dad, that his father hadn't cared for him in the same way that his mom had, but Clarence had still loved him, wanted to make him proud. Maybe Lucy seemed so alone because she thought her mother hated her and her dad wasn't around. It was good that they had figured things out.

Lucy missed her dad, too. There might be some guilt in there, for missing her father but being angry because he wasn't around. It seemed like she'd latched onto Clarence so that she'd stop thinking about her bad feelings.

She was in his apartment.

Clarence couldn't think of an explanation for that.

That meant that her mother was in his apartment as well.

She'd said that she was trying to trick him. Her voice had sounded small, far away.

He'd just lost his job.

In revenge, he'd just locked his ex-boss in a closet with his germs.

Clarence shook his head, trying to mute the string of thoughts. He hadn't finished cleaning the apartment this morning. That would settle his turbulent mind. Checking his watch, he smiled. He could also watch the last half hour of the 6 o' clock news. He reached for the remote on the coffee table, saw the can next to it, and the bottle and glass on the floor. He gathered them up to take them to the kitchen, but stopped and turned the TV on.

"—that he was, in fact, a victim and not the perpetrator," the female news anchor said. "Richard

Monroe refused to comment, but his lawyer spoke on behalf of his client this afternoon."

Clarence came back into the living room.

On the screen was a man in a crisp suit. "I'd like to say that Mr. Monroe is relieved to be found innocent, but he is still left without a wife and daughter, and relief seems beyond his present circumstances."

The screen changed again. It was file footage, not live, because it was a day-time shot, and the sun had already set. Clarence's legs lost feeling and he collapsed onto the arm of the chair. Unable to hold himself steady, he tipped over and sprawled onto the seat of the chair.

Over the stock footage of Clarence's apartment building, the news anchor said, "Mr. Monroe's lawyer refused further comment, and his client couldn't be reached. The court documents are sealed, so we may never know the true story of an event that rocked this apartment complex in one of the safest neighborhoods in Detroit."

She spoke with excessive emphasis, pausing after each phrase, and Clarence wanted to break through the TV screen and shake her, yelling at her to hurry up, he needed more information. Although the file footage showed his entire building, he clearly saw his red front door in the center. He needed to know more.

Instead, the screen changed to show the two anchors and the meteorologist, who was standing in front of a map with what Clarence presumed to be the current area temperatures.

"People are in for a cold, wet surprise for their morning commute, huh, Andrew?" she said while the male anchor grimaced jovially.

"That's right," the meteorologist said. "We're tracking a system that—"

Clarence hit the pause button on his remote, then rewind. The DVR time-bar on the bottom of the screen backed up three minutes, to the time when Clarence turned on the TV.

"—that he was, in fact, a victim and not the perpetrator."

"No!" Clarence wrung the remote, then stabbed the rewind button.

"—that he was, in fact—"

Clarence drew his arm back to throw the remote at the TV, but then just turned it off. Biting his lip for a moment, he hurried into his office, turned on the computer, tapping his foot while he waited for it to boot up.

When he finally was able to open Google, he typed "Richard Monroe."

The first article was titled *Applewood Apartments Double Homicide*. He clicked on the link.

It had initially been believed that Victoria Monroe had caught her husband after he'd drowned their daughter in the bathtub of their Applewood apartment. He'd attacked her, at which point she'd run to the kitchen and managed to get a paring knife, which she'd used to try and fight him off. Victoria had stabbed him in the shoulder, where the blade had gotten caught in the joint and snapped, leaving only about an inch behind. The police investigation concluded that Richard had continued his assault, despite being stabbed with the broken knife several more times, until he was finally able to wrestle it away from Victoria, at which point he used it to slash his wife's left forearm and then dumped her in the tub with their dead daughter. Then he'd tried to flee the scene, but lost consciousness on his way out of the apartment due to his multiple stab wounds which, although shallow, bled copiously.

Clarence, leaning forward in his chair so that his face was inches from the screen, scanned the rest of the article, but it didn't give the daughter a name. He backed up a page and clicked another article, *Face of Innocence*.

The text of the article loaded before the image.

The coroner who had performed the autopsies concluded that Lucy Monroe had died between 3 and 5 P.M. Witnesses testified that Richard Monroe had left work at five on the dot, like he did every day. Given distance and presumed rush hour traffic, Richard wouldn't have gotten home until at least 5:30 P.M. That had cleared him of his daughter's murder, but not his wife's.

The image link was broken. Clarence inhaled sharply through clenched teeth and seized the monitor with both hands. That wouldn't help, so he forced himself to calm down and keep reading.

After the time of death had been established for Lucy Monroe, the prosecution's angle shifted to

Richard murdering his wife in the heat of passion. He'd come home to find his daughter drowned in the bathtub. Believing that his wife had killed their daughter, Richard had attacked her. Getting away from him, she'd gone to the kitchen and gotten the paring knife to defend herself, stabbing Richard twenty-seven times before he could wrestle the knife away. Then he killed her, dumped her in the tub, tried to flee, lost consciousness, and the neighbors called the police because of the noise.

Called to the stand, Richard had told his version about a depressed housewife whose passivity changed to aggression.

Richard had come home from work that day and walked past his wife, who was sitting on the couch, on his way to the bathroom. Once there, he'd found his daughter drowned, come back to confront Victoria, who then attacked him with a knife. He'd tried his best to defend himself without hurting her, finally losing consciousness because of blood loss. He hadn't even known that his wife was also dead until he'd woken up in the hospital the next day. He'd assumed that she committed suicide out of regret, or fear of the consequences of her actions, or maybe it had been her plan all along.

The two stories were almost identical, but after the coroner testified to Richard's almost certain innocence in the murder of his daughter, he was cross-examined to provide insight into how Victoria Monroe had died.

The coroner had claimed that it was most

likely, evidenced by the angle and path of the deep cut in her left forearm which severed five veins and two arteries, that Victoria had committed suicide. To slash her arm like that, Richard would have needed to stand behind her, reach across her body with his right hand, and pull the knife up and to the right. The coroner also concluded that it was most likely that the wound was inflicted while Victoria was already in the tub, since she had been found cradling her daughter, both arms limply around her. That arrangement represented considerable trouble for Richard. Despite his blood loss at that time, Richard would have needed to remove his daughter's body, put his wife's in, replace his daughter's and then wrap his wife's arms around her.

After an hour and forty-five minutes of deliberation, the jury had decided that that was highly unlikely and found Richard Monroe not guilty.

Clarence searched through several articles, reading the same information over and over.

Finally, he found a picture of Lucy Monroe.

His Lucy stared at him from his computer screen. She looked different, younger. Her cheeks were a little pudgier and her hair was shorter and straighter, but the same shade of jet black. She looked too serious to be so young.

In the family portrait, she was sitting in her mother's lap. Lucy strongly resembled her mother, but Victoria's face was too pale, slack and saggy. Her arms limply held her daughter just like when she'd cut her wrist.

Clarence looked away, making a guttural sound as he tried not to throw up. After a few moments, he was able to look back and study Victoria's face.

Yes, there was some passing resemblance to his mother, especially near the end, when she'd been confined to the hospital bed. Victoria looked sick, worn out, and even though her hair was black and his mother's had been chestnut brown, Clarence could have easily mistaken the color as she'd emerged from the shadowed hallway, IV tubes dangling from her arm.

Except they had been her severed veins and arteries.

This time, Clarence bolted from his office, across the hall, wrenching the toilet seat up. He dry-heaved, his stomach muscles clenching, nothing coming up except a little bile. He hadn't eaten anything since yesterday.

Clarence spat into the toilet, flushed, then got up to brush his teeth. He stopped and turned. Staring down at the tub, he felt his stomach twist again, and gritted his teeth against the urge. He wanted to find out for sure which apartment the Monroes had lived in, but he needed to brush his teeth first. After all, stomach acid was six times more corrosive than cola.

Nearing exhaustion, Clarence went to the living room, and realized that he hadn't finished cleaning the apartment. Even worse, he'd been surfing for information for more than an hour while his germs multiplied and spread onto surfaces that he'd cleaned earlier. He gathered up the bottle of ammonia and the roll of paper towels and started toward the closet, but then stopped, remembering why he had come in here in the first place. He walked back to the table and the phone, but didn't pick it up because his hands were full of things that needed to be put away. His pulse throbbed in his temples. Juggling the bottle and the towels with the phone, he managed to call Bob O'Neill.

It rang four times, connected, then a recorded woman's pleasant voice said, "Hello, you've reached the Applewood Apartments' business office. Bob O'Neill, the apartments' manager, is away from his desk at the moment. Our normal business hours are 8 A.M. to 5 P.M. Monday through Friday; 1 to 5 P.M. on Saturdays. Please leave your name, number and a brief message and we'll get back to you as soon as we're able."

Clarence had put away the ammonia, gotten out the Lysol Multi-Surface, and started wiping down the tables, shelves and TV. He'd already known that Bob wouldn't be in the office. He just needed the emergency number.

"In case of an emergency…"

He repeated the number, then again, and a third time while he dried the TV screen. He hung up on the answering machine and dialed the emergency number.

Bob picked up on the second ring. "Bob O'Neill."

"Hello, Mr. O'Neill, it's Clarence Gottlieb from building two, apartment 4."

There was a slight hesitation. "Hi, Clarence.

What can I do for you this evening?"

"Did the Monroes live in my apartment?"

Silence from Bob. Clarence couldn't even hear him breathing.

"I'm sorry to be calling like this," he explained. "I just got home from work—actually I was just fired—and I saw this news story. I'd never heard of him before. Richard Monroe, that is. That's not usually the sort of story I pay attention to. But they were talking about the crime and they showed Applewood, my building—my door was in the center. I—"

"Did someone harass you for an interview?"

"What? No. But my door…"

"Yes." Bob drew the word out, which tickled Clarence's ear, making him shudder. "Could you come by the office tomorrow? This is something that I think we should talk about, man-to-man, face-to-face. Is that okay?"

Clarence sputtered. "I—I just need to know if he—they—lived in this apartment."

"Tomorrow—"

"No! Now!"

Bob O'Neill sighed, a long sound which made Clarence want to grab hold of his hands, touch his face, push his fingers into his mouth, infect him and then watch him suffer.

Finally, he said, "Yes."

"They lived here?"

"Yes. They lived there."

Bob O'Neill started to say something else, but Clarence didn't hear him. Dumbstruck, he hung up the phone, dropped the Lysol and paper towel, wandered to his bathroom.

Except, it had been their bathroom.

This was where she'd done it. Right here. Held Lucy's head under the water, her daughter's struggles getting weaker, weaker, her arms splashing limply into the water. Taken Lucy into her arms, cradled her, and slashed her left arm. The coroner had said that it was likely that the water had still been warm when Victoria committed suicide. She'd exhibited no signs of traumatic blood loss, had simply and peacefully waited to die.

His shock snapped, and Clarence bolted to the front closet, grabbed all the cleaning products he had, and ran back to the bathroom. From under the sink, he pulled everything else and started spraying, splashing, pouring chemicals on the walls, sides, and floor of the shower. He scrubbed each chemical in with a new brush which he threw away after a full pass from top to bottom.

He didn't rinse between applications, not wanting to dilute the chemicals' cleaning power. Splashing bleach from the bottle up onto the walls, he started to feel dizzy immediately. Staggering back, he almost lost consciousness, but didn't let himself. He needed to finish.

Scouring between deep, held breaths, his eyes watered, his vision graying around the edges, but he was almost done. Just needed to do around the drain, and no, he didn't hear her voice, her crying. He wouldn't.

Finally, he turned the hot water all the way on, rinsed the shower. The rising steam dispersed the deadly mixed chemicals even more effectively, and Clarence sagged on his feet, losing strength.

Eventually, he was able to breathe easier, but the pounding headache didn't go away. In the other room, the phone rang. Clarence almost obeyed his compulsion to go answer it, but all he could do was stand there, residual dizziness and increasing nausea making him sway widely.

"Help me," she said, not from the drain, but all around him. As it grew fainter, he couldn't help but think that she was being washed down the pipes and away. "Help me. Help me. You promised to…"

19

The apartment was a mess.

Not just a mess. That implied that things weren't where they belonged; that the chaos existed only in the moratorium before order was restored. Such was not the case.

Recognizable elements were scattered around: books that probably belonged on bookshelves which had been smashed to pieces; pots and pans strewn down the hallway to the bedrooms; one half of the table stood propped up by two umbrellas in the dining area, the other half had been taken apart methodically, the screwdriver and wrench still sitting next to the pieces, the screws and bolts long gone. The two-bedroom apartment had been destroyed, like a revenging tornado had ripped through it.

Yet, Clarence felt oddly calm.

It was the furniture, or what could be identified as what had once been furniture. This couch was cream with baby blue stripes; not his. The dining room table was natural wood finish with white trim and legs; also not his. The book that he picked up was Danielle Steele.

But he was certain that it was his apartment. The walls were the same golden yellow that had charmed him when he'd first walked through the door with Bob O'Neill.

He'd called Bob yesterday. For something. About the apartment.

His eyes widening and his mouth dropping open, he vaulted over the shards and pieces of a glass-topped coffee table. "Lucy?" he called as loudly as he dared. "Lucy, where are you? I'm here to… I'm here!"

She wasn't in her room, the bathroom or any of the closets. She wasn't hiding in any of the cabinets in the kitchen, under or behind anything. Clarence even checked the stove and the refrigerator, yelping and then laughing shakily when he found Ducky sitting in a roasting pan in the freezer.

The door of the master bedroom was shut.

Approaching cautiously, he tried to picture Victoria, not as the woman who'd scared him, but as the woman he'd seen in that one family portrait, who she'd been. She'd probably been the one who had picked the colors of the apartment, the rich yellow living and dining rooms, the subtle lavender of Lucy's bedroom, the alternating glossy-flat striped red of the bedroom she'd shared with her husband. Of course he'd liked the front rooms, they were his favorite color, but he'd been surprised by the master bedroom. Whoever had come up with the technique of alternating finishes had been quite clever, he'd thought, and it had been her.

Clarence's mom had done all the cooking. So had Victoria, in all likelihood. He'd always smelled the cooking food long before it was ready, and he pictured Lucy coming out of her room as he had, wandering into the kitchen, asking when dinner would be done.

His mom had always tried to shoo him away, but if he hung around long enough, he'd get to taste things for her, help her decide if it needed more of something. As he got older, his mom would tell him that dinner would be ready sooner if he helped, so he started making the salads, telling her about school while they worked. He figured that Lucy was smart enough to learn that trick of persistence as well, and was sure that she'd gotten many small spoonfuls that had teased her appetite.

Clarence put his hand on the doorknob.

Once he'd reached double digits, his parents had started sleeping with their door shut at night. He'd been old enough, they said, to get his own glass of water if he got thirsty, and to not come running into their room because of nightmare monsters. They were just make-believe things that couldn't hurt him. Still, the monsters came back from time to time, and he would wake up and call for his mom, who would come into his room, talk to him for a few minutes, soothe whatever fear he had, then shut herself behind a door again. At first, he'd been angry at her for leaving him alone. Then, she had died, he'd felt guilty and realized that she'd been trying to teach him how to be self-reliant. Lucy was still young enough that she probably didn't see and understand the bigger picture as Victoria did, but someday, given enough time and distance, she'd gain that perspective, as Clarence had.

Except she wouldn't.

Because she was dead.

Clarence had been twisting the doorknob, but now eased it back. Victoria was nothing like his mom, and he needed to remember that.

Maybe Victoria had Lucy in the room right now, holding her tightly with one hand over her mouth. Lucy would still be struggling; Clarence knew that much about her. He pressed his ear against the door, listening hard.

There… He thought… A sound, like a muffled cry. Clarence burst into the room, not sure what he would do, but certain that he couldn't do nothing.

The room was empty.

He stood, concentrating, only heard the pounding of his heart and the rushing sound his pulse made in his ears.

The room made him sad. The mirror over the dresser had been broken, the drawers taken out and the body of it smashed. The mattress and box spring had been cut open, the fabric discarded like shed skin and springs littered the floor. The headboard and another dresser had been pushed up against the single window in the room, blocking it, making an open space in the middle of the room that was filled with pictures, pieces of pictures. Half-faces stared up at him, decapitated torsos, arms with scratched-out hands, blurred backgrounds collaged together.

Clarence backed out of the room, closing the door. He felt small as he turned and walked back into the living room.

It seemed almost silly to clean up in the midst of this devastation, and the idea of his germs spreading seemed unimportant. Nevertheless, he couldn't help himself. He organized the books into neat piles. He wrestled the couch right side up, pushed it against the wall where the couch sat in his apartment, this apartment, not his apartment. Unable to find the screws and bolts to put it back together, Clarence finished taking the dining table apart, then gathered the pots and pans from the hallway and took them back to the kitchen. He folded the clothes that he found in the cupboards, taking the little girl clothes back to the lavender bedroom, the grown-up clothes to the red striped one. Clarence stood in the doorway, unsure of what to do with them. Finally, he pushed his way through the broken shards of dresser and sorted the clothes into the drawers, which had been stacked on one side of the room.

Returning to the living room, he brushed by a precariously tall stack of books. They teetered, fell, causing a small avalanche and Clarence's shoulders slumped.

There was no point, to any of it. Cleaning things that just got dirty again. Working to contain his germs when scientists weaponized lethal viruses, and even that didn't matter because people died anyway, died alone. In the end, everyone died alone, the people who actually cared ripped away to be replaced by staring eyes behind anonymous masks and screeching machinery.

Better to just let go and let things end.

Clarence started restacking the books.

Bent over at the waist, gathering them up with one hand and holding them in a stack against his body with his other arm, he stopped. One book, this one by

Alexa Rohls, was sitting on an angle, propped up by nothing. Clarence reached forward, touching the book with his finger, trying to push it over. It wouldn't budge.

Straightening up, Clarence took a step back. There was an empty space in the middle of the room, a little closer to the kitchen. Clarence realized that he had walked past this empty space about half a dozen times, unconsciously avoiding it each time. Clarence held out the stack of books, let them fall. Like he expected, they cascaded to either side of the empty space, creating the form of an amorphous blob with two pseudo-pods like legs pointed toward the living room.

Clarence jerked back, stumbling into the couch.

Richard.

This was where the police had found Richard unconscious when they'd broken down the door. He was still here, a part of him anyway. A memory of the people who lived here, as unformed as a world made of gray fog.

"Clarence! Thank goodness!" she said from behind him.

He whirled, but she was across the room, her arms wrapped around him before he could get a good look at her. Victoria seemed so different from how he had pictured her that he didn't know what to do, so he patted her on the back as she pushed her face into his chest and nuzzled his neck.

His arms were strong around her; he smelled so clean. Rubbing her hands up and down his back, she inhaled deeply, exhaling in a drawn-out sigh. Things would be better now, for all of them. She pulled away from him, so she could stand on her tip toes, kiss him.

Clarence tried to recoil as she craned her neck back, her face up, her pale lips puckering. She was so pale, her skin gray. Her black hair was wet, plastered against her skull. Her clothes were dripping and had made the front of his body cold and clammy. Still, she clutched his arms.

He was so warm, and she had been chilled to the bone for she couldn't remember how long. He seemed hesitant, but that didn't matter. She knew what men wanted. One hand sliding up his neck to pull his face down to hers, the other glided along the front of his body, over his chest, his stomach, down.

Clarence held her wrist, trying to pry loose from her grip on his hair when her other hand brushed the front of his pants. Almost immediately, his lower stomach tightened and his hips thrust forward. She moaned in satisfaction against his mouth and he blushed. His clenched jaw relaxed, his lips parted and her tongue slipped between his teeth and into his mouth. It was cold and violent as it lashed against his.

Clarence tore away from her, gagging, confused. Staggering back, he nearly tripped over the empty spot on the floor. "Richard," he blurted.

Her eyes narrowed and she frowned for just a moment before smiling again, stepping forward. "He left us."

Clarence glanced around. "Lucy. Where's Lucy?"

She shushed him. “There will be time for her.” Her fingers traced the side of his face, the severed blood vessels swinging with her slow movements. “After.”

Clarence’s shoulder hit the wall as he shrank away from her touch. Ricocheting off, he stumbled into the hallway leading to the bedrooms. Victoria pressed forward, herding him. Arms out straight, he clamped down on her shoulders, stopping her.

She moved slowly, rolling her hips. It had been so long, too long, and it would be so lovely. Then, he grabbed her and she felt a rush of desire. That was the one thing she’d always asked Richard to do that he never did: take control, show her that he wanted her, needed her. She closed her eyes, tilted her head back, smiling lips parting, her breath caught in her throat.

She seemed to enjoy his tightly squeezed hands on her, which scared him. Pushing her away, he needed to catch her, holding her upright when she almost lost her balance. Back out into the living room, he let go and went to stand on the other side of the room with the deconstructed table between them.

“Where’s Lucy?”

Victoria blinked, shivered without his warmth, and crossed her arms over her chest. “She ran away.”

Looking around, Clarence asked, “What happened?”

“Same thing that always happens,” she said. “She was being a little monster and when I tried to show her that she couldn’t act like that, she started crying, like I’m the bad guy for trying to raise her right."

He would understand. Richard hadn't because he was weak. Clarence was strong. Victoria slunk around the table while he was lost in thought. Putting a hand on his back, she tried nudging him toward the bedroom again.

He didn't notice that she'd moved until she was right next to him. Clarence shied away and moved across the living room toward the dining area. He needed to think. Lucy had run away. She was probably lost in the fog, waiting for him. He needed to go find her—but then what?

"Now that you're here, you can help me," she whispered into his ear.

Clarence hadn't seen her move. She was across the room one moment, then next to him.

"Help me," she said. "I don't want the world to be gray anymore. I want to look out the window and see blue sky, sunshine, the wind rustling the leaves."

He tried to get away from her again, but now she was on the other side of him and he put his arms around her to keep her from falling and she tangled her fingers in his hair, pulling his glasses off.

"You can make it how it was supposed to be. Then, she'll come back, because she likes you, and she'll see how it is, and then you and I can raise her together, raise her right." Her lips found his neck, her breath tickling the sensitive skin.

Clarence tried to let go, but Victoria held on too tight. Squeezing his arms between their bodies, he pushed. She didn't fall backward, but released him, her face contorting.

"So that's it then?" she demanded. "You're just going to abandon us."

Clarence's stomach clenched with guilt. "No, it's just—"

"It's your fault, you know. She never ran away before. She didn't always listen to me, but at least she listened to me about that. And then you come along, and you think that taking her to the park once makes you her friend. Well now she's lost, and I don't know where she is and can't you see I'm worried sick and you won't even help me?"

His heart pounded, and the world around him started losing definition. At the same time, he thought he could smell the sharp tang of bleach, feel the cold tile on his right side.

Clarence fought with all his concentration to stay here. He needed to find Lucy first, tell her everything would be alright, that he'd be back for her, would keep coming back for her.

When he opened his eyes, Victoria was on the floor, her arms wrapped around his legs. "No please, no please," she was saying. Sensing a change, she looked up at him, laughed shakily. "I knew you wouldn't leave me. You're not like him."

He broke loose from her grasp. "I'm going to go find Lucy," he said.

Her eyes narrowed and her lips tightened. Standing, she lunged forward. Clarence gasped, feeling the stinging pain in his hand and seeing the red drops of blood follow the arc of the knife she held. Victoria snarled, waved the knife in front of her face and he saw that its blade was broken, only an inch or so remaining.

Clarence looked down at his hand. It was smeared with crimson, but wasn't cut. This was just a dream.

Clarence tried to push past her, but she struck at him again and he winced, the stinging in his face already fading, gone. Putting his hands out to ward her off, he stepped forward.

Slashing out at him again, she fought against a dark feeling of worthlessness. Of course he wanted her; his mind was simply too occupied with Lucy missing. She wanted to drop the knife, apologize, explain, like she had tried to explain to Richard.

"It will be better now that you're here."

Clarence tried to maneuver around her, either to the front door or the sliding glass patio door. Every time he shifted his weight, though, she blocked him, cut him. It stung only for a moment, but he instinctively shrank away.

"You'll see."

He leaned left, then dodged back to the right when she swung the knife. Jumping over the arm of the couch, he sprinted for the patio door, but then she was there in front of him. He couldn't believe it. She shoved him and he tripped over a pile of books and fell.

"This world isn't for us. She's gone ahead. She's waiting."

Victoria's eyes were glazed as she leaned over

him. Kneeling down, her face was inches from his, her eyes miles away.

"Come with us. It'll be how it was meant to be."

Clarence jerked to the side and Victoria lost her balance. Rising, he bolted back toward the bedrooms. Behind him, from the front door, he heard her growl.

She stood in front of the door, clutching the knife in frustration. Instead of the front door, he ran down the hallway. Blinking, she stood in the doorway of her bedroom, the one she'd shared with Richard that she'd soon share with Clarence. Her arm out, the knife extended, she braced herself.

Clarence saw her standing in the doorway of the bedroom and pivoted left, into Lucy's room. Without thinking, he barreled toward the window, shielding his face. He crashed into it, the impact sending tremors up his arms, the crunching sound of his elbows breaking the glass. Then, he was outside, half-propped up by the bush under the window. Scrambling, he pulled his legs through the window, kicking back when he felt her grabbing at him.

The fog had pushed back when he'd crashed through the window and she looked at the lawn, the parking lot, the trees, the other apartment buildings and houses across the street. To the left was the intersection of Grand River and Outer Drive, empty, but there. Victoria laughed, real, genuine laughter for the first time in she couldn't remember how long. Things would be perfect now and forever. Clarence would give them the world, and she'd give him everything in return.

The blue sky grayed, the clouds rushing down and sweeping along the streets. Clarence had disappeared. Victoria howled, slicing the curtains, the air, herself.

Clarence could almost hear her. After he'd staggered free of the bushes, his first thought had been of Lucy. There was only one place she could have gone.

He stood at the edge of the park, looking across the playground at the trees where he and Mickey had spent so many hours.

Except now it wasn't summer, it was November. The trees were bare, the grass was brittle and stiff under his feet. Through the bare branches, he saw her, she saw him, and she leapt down, both of them running toward each other.

After Lucy had run blindly out the front door of the apartment and into the fog, she'd tried to focus on Clarence's park. Shapes had coalesced in the fog, but dissipated when she'd run toward them. On the brink of tears, she put all her effort into picturing the tree that she'd sat in with Clarence, the rustle of the leaves, the rough bark, and there it was. Except it didn't look like she remembered it. This was a winter tree, its branches bare, cold. She'd climbed it anyway, struggling to get up without a boost. Shivering against the cold, she'd waited.

The first thing she noticed changing was that there was now grass at the base of the tree. Then, another tree, the one that Mickey had sat in. The driveway that ran along the park, the playground equipment. Then, she saw him across the field and she jumped down, ran, flung herself into his waiting arms and started crying.

"Shh," he said, trying to run his fingers through her wet hair. She shivered against him.

"Don't—leave. Don—don't leave. Prom—ise you'll—st—stay with me."

"I can't," he said. "I can't. But I'll be back. I'll always come back."

Lucy shook her head, started pushing him away, hitting his chest when he tried to hold her.

"No. No. You have to stay. Promise you'll—stay!"

Clarence couldn't think of anything to say, any way that he could explain what had happened to her, why he couldn't stay.

Instead, he tried to distract her. "Hey!" he said, reaching into his pocket. "Want some Sour Patch?"

She snuffled, and stopped struggling. She didn't say yes, but she held out her hand when he pulled the bag out. Clarence wiped her face with a tissue as she ate the candy.

The silence between them was too painful, so he said without thinking, "What happened? The mess, at the apartment."

Lucy wailed, collapsing to the ground. Clarence gathered her up and rocked her, stroking her hair, humming softly. His mother had always hummed to him when he'd been upset, and somehow that small sound had penetrated his mind in a way that comforting words couldn't.

But Lucy would not be calmed. She cried until he became worried that she would hurt herself somehow. Then, the crying tapered off. He held her without speaking, unsure what to say.

"She hurt me again," Lucy whispered. "It was just like that time I tried to set her free by breaking the mirror. Except this time, I couldn't get away down the drain. The water stung my eyes, my mouth, my nose."

"So you ran away," Clarence said.

"She held me down a long time, and I couldn't get away, so I started scratching her arm. She let go and I ran."

He hugged her, rocked her, said nothing, realized that he couldn't feel her in his arms. She was fading, along with the world around him. This time, he couldn't stop it.

"Promise you'll stay," Lucy said, even as Clarence set her down on the ground that was turning gray, becoming fog.

"I'm sorry," he said. He couldn't see her anymore. Reaching forward to pat her head reassuringly, his fingers trailed wisps of fog and touched nothing.

Lucy sat alone in the gray world. Even the tree was gone. She felt too tired to cry, wanted to lie down, close her eyes and for this to all be a bad dream.

Sitting up sharply, she squinted, trying to see through the haze. A dark blot colored the near horizon, and she got up and approached it cautiously. Another shape bruised the light gray.

"There you are!" her mother sang, grabbing her by the arm. Lucy didn't struggle. "Well?"

Lucy shook her head, as if it wasn't obvious that Clarence was gone.

Her mother grunted. "Well, let's see if we can make the matter a bit more pressing," she said, dragging Lucy into the apartment.

Tuesday

20

Clarence shifted, his back stiff from spending the night on the hard tile of the bathroom. His head pounded almost as bad as yesterday. He couldn't remember if he'd hit it on the way to the floor. It was kind of blurry.

Sitting up, he heard sounds coming from the living room. Of course. He'd left the TV on. He'd been watching the news.

His stomach growled because he hadn't had anything to eat since Sunday. When he thought of food, his stomach rushed up to churn behind his throat and he put it as far out of his mind as he could. Squirming over to the wall, he sat up against it, his vision pulsing with each movement.

Clarence winced. It penetrated his foggy brain that he was hearing knocking at the door of his apartment, not just his headache. He braced his hands on his knees and slid up the wall, his legs shaking. Accidentally kicking a spray-bottle of Lysol Tub & Tile out of the way, he stumbled out of the bathroom.

Looking out the peephole on the door, he saw a man staring straight back, like he expected to be able to see into the apartment. The man had on a black parka and hat with earflaps. Leaving the chain on, Clarence opened the door.

"Mr. Gottlieb?" the man asked even before Clarence could say hello.

"Yes. Can I help you?"

"I'm Detective Andrew Brennen, Detroit Police. Mind if I ask you a few questions?"

Clarence hesitated. He didn't know how long he'd been unconscious, how long his germs had been multiplying and spreading. "I'm sorry, um—my apartment's a real mess right now."

Detective Brennen's eyes narrowed. "It's awful cold out here, Mr. Gottlieb. If your apartment is too much of a mess right now, I can give you a ride back to the precinct. We can chat there."

"No, no. That won't be necessary," Clarence said, though he made no move to undo the chain. "Can you tell me what this is about?"

The detective tried to look past the man into his apartment, but he moved to block his view. Brennen didn't think the place was a mess from what he saw. The man was hiding something. His face was puffy and bruised, especially his nose, which looked like it could be broken. Not enough for probable cause, given what this guy's co-worker had said about him.

"We're investigating the death of James Caruthers. He was your boss, is that correct?"

Gottlieb's face went slack and he sagged against the door. His arm fell limp from where it had been supporting him against the doorframe. If the door hadn't been chained, the detective could have used this opportunity to brush by him into the apartment, technically not breaking the rules of investigation.

Shivering, he nonetheless allowed Gottlieb time to process what he'd said.

"Mr. Caruthers." Clarence bit his upper lip. "Is dead?"

"Heart attack," the detective said. "Coroner thinks between five and seven, but we have witnesses that put him alive at five fifteen."

Brennen watched his suspect carefully.

"Funny thing is," he continued, "he was found in the closet of his office. What time did you say you got to work yesterday?"

Gottlieb blinked, like he just remembered that he was talking to someone.

"Uh—I was late," Clarence said. "I, uh—didn't… didn't see…" He could feel his face turning red with his feeble attempt at lying.

"Found some paperwork on the desk." Brennen held up a termination form, signed. "Got any idea what this is?"

Clarence hung his head, sorry that he'd even tried. His mom would be ashamed of him.

He nodded.

Detective Brennen smiled. He hadn't expected this to go so easily. "We're going to need you to come to the precinct, testify as to your involvement with yesterday's events."

Clarence's breath hitched in his throat. "Am I under—under arrest?"

Brennen pursed his lips. He didn't have a warrant, had come out here only on a hunch. The most popular theory at the station was that Caruthers had somehow gotten trapped in the closet and had had a panic-induced heart attack. But the two janitors that Brennen had talked to had told him about what had happened on Sunday. There was also the termination form sitting on the desk.

"James Caruthers died of a heart attack," Brennen said. "We're just trying to put all the pieces together."

Clarence steadied, though his lower lip still quivered. "So, I'm not under arrest."

Not wanting to answer the question, he asked, "Does the name Valerie Hendricks mean anything to you?"

He hadn't quite expected Clarence's reaction, so was left slack-jawed when Clarence yelped and slammed the door in his face. Balling a fist, he pounded on the door.

"Gottlieb, I can come back with a warrant!" No answer. He pounded again, notebook crushed is his other hand. "Gottlieb?" Pausing, he put his ear closer to the door, knocked softer. It sounded thick, like Gottlieb was leaning against the other side. Listening carefully, he heard muffled words, but couldn't make anything out. "You can make this easier on all of us."

Clarence, his back against the door, groaned and shook his head, hands on his face. Doubling over, he tried to put his head between his knees, but couldn't bend down that far. Nausea swam in his battered stomach.

"I'm sorry Mom," he was repeating, the words that Brennen couldn't quite hear.

He had murdered Mr. Caruthers, just like he'd murdered his mom. Except, his mom had died because he'd been careless. Mr. Caruthers had died by Clarence's will. He'd spread his germs in that closet. He'd locked his boss inside. He'd stood there, listening to his struggles until they stopped, and then, he'd walked away.

It had been the same with his mom. He'd been there, standing by her bedside, when the machines that tracked her life in impersonal beeps had started shrieking. His father had needed to pull him out of the room, because otherwise, he would have watched, watched as the doctors did all they could, finally giving up, pulling the sheet up over her face.

He'd tried to tell his father, confess what he'd done. All his father had said was "Don't be stupid."

Nobody had blamed him for his mom's death, but the police were outside his door. He thought he could still hear the detective, grunting and whispering, but he didn't dare shift his weight against the door to check through the peephole. Clarence barely breathed, trying to be as quiet as possible, his head spinning.

He'd lied to a policeman. His mom had told him that the police were as good as parents, and now he'd lied, shut the door on him. Clarence's face burned, and his vision grayed again.

It had been the same with Lucy.

She'd looked up at him, her heart in her eyes, and begged him to stay with her, tried to make him promise. Except instead of just standing there, he'd left.

It wasn't the same though. He'd woken up. That wasn't the same as walking away and leaving Mr. Caruthers to die.

Maybe if he'd opened the closet door, he would have seen that something was seriously wrong and taken him to a hospital.

Clarence had allowed himself to wake up. When Victoria had yelled at him, cut him, he had fought to stay there. He'd wanted to find Lucy, tell her everything would be alright. But when he'd found her, and realized that things needed to be made alright, he'd left her.

He hadn't even promised he'd be back. He said he'd come back, but he hadn't promised. The last words he'd said to her were "I'm sorry."

Mr. Caruthers hadn't even gotten that much.

Neither had his mom.

Neither had Val, and all she'd done was try to be his friend.

His hands on his knees, Clarence pushed himself up. He closed his eyes, breathed deep. His stomach hardened against the rolling nausea and his vision was clear when he looked around the apartment.

It was a mess. All of his best efforts had been for nothing. His mother was dead. Mr. Caruthers was dead. Val would never be his friend.

Lucy was still trying, and he wouldn't let her down.

Turning around, he looked through the peephole. Detective Brennen had gone.

Grabbing his coat and hat, he walked out, down

the walk to his car. He hadn't cleaned the knob or the lock. Someone, probably the mailman, would come along, pick up his germs, spread them to his co-workers, then take them home. His stomach knotted with the need to go back and protect the world from his germs.

Except this was more important. He got into his car and drove.

21

Up to Six Mile, then across to Livernois, his old neighborhood. He hadn't been here in years, not since cleaning out his parents' house after his father died. He fought against the old habit to pull into the driveway of the house, but a metallic orange minivan was parked there, a reminder that this wasn't his place anymore. He drove up to the curb next to the house next door and turned off the car, got out. Patting his pockets, he compromised by wiping the handle clean.

An eerie sense of déjà vu tilted the ground beneath his feet. It was long moments before he could steady himself, realizing that this is where he'd stood, looking across the park, the playground, and saw Lucy sitting in his tree.

He kept his steps slow and deliberate. There were a few children playing in the park, chaperoned by an older woman huddled inside her coat, sitting on a bench. He didn't want to draw their attention. He was just a man strolling down memory lane.

They didn't seem to notice him as he crossed the park and walked up to the trees lining the driveway.

Standing with his neck craned, he called softly, "Lucy."

There was no one up in the tree.

"Lucy," he called again, a little louder.

He thought about climbing the tree, but rejected that idea almost immediately. Grown men didn't climb trees. The woman over at the playground would think he was crazy.

Circling the trunk, Clarence listened hard. A few days ago, when he'd been in the bathroom, the sink had started backing up for no reason. Lucy had done that. There'd also been that empty spot in the living room where Richard wasn't. As Clarence came back around the tree, he searched the branches, the ground for any sign of disturbance, something that was there, but wasn't.

Not seeing her, he called her name again.

Going around in widening circles, he passed Mickey's tree.

"Lucy. Lucy. Lucy. Mick—"

He stopped, looked over his shoulder. Mickey wasn't up there, was probably married with children by now. They hadn't spoken in years, not since they went to different high schools after middle school. The other night, they hadn't spoken. Mickey had just been there as part of the dream, which was also part-memory. But Lucy had been there.

Looking down at the ground, Clarence's brow creased.

Yes, Lucy had been there. He hadn't known Lucy had existed until last week, hadn't known that she had lived in his apartment, that she'd been drowned in his bathtub, so many things he hadn't known that proved that she wasn't a figment of his imagination or memory like Mickey had been.

Still, Clarence had called up to Mickey's tree, empty now that the boy had grown up, expecting his friend to answer.

Like he expected Lucy to answer him.

She had to be here. There was nowhere else for her to go.

"Excuse me?"

Clarence whirled, his lips moving. He'd been calling Lucy's name over and over, only noticing because he'd fallen silent under the concerned gaze of the woman from the bench.

"Yes?" Clarence said, shakily.

"I don't think your daughter is in any of the trees. Did you check around the building?"

Clarence looked at the community center that the driveway led to. The woman sounded so sure of herself, he thought he might see Lucy come running around the corner of the building any moment. Then, he remembered that that was ridiculous.

"No, I'm sure she isn't over there. I don't think I dreamed that part."

The woman's eyebrows rose, but she said, "Lucy… is your daughter's name?"

"Oh, she's not my daughter," Clarence said. "She's a friend. She ran away from home but then I woke up."

The woman nodded slowly. Clarence smiled, happy that he'd found someone so sympathetic to him.

"I think you need to move on now, sir." Her words were short, clipped.

Clarence blinked twice. "I'm sorry?"

"This is a nice neighborhood. There's a shelter over on Livernois that can help you."

The two children that had been playing on the playground stood behind the woman, one peeking out from around either leg. Clarence looked down at them, and they shied away. The woman's lips were a thin, tight line. Her arms were folded across her chest.

He'd been calling for someone who wasn't there. She'd asked questions—what they'd been he couldn't remember, nor his answers. He still felt nauseous and a little dizzy. He also couldn't remember showering today. Shuffling away from the three people in front of him, his sudden movement made the kids jump and the woman uncross her arms to hold her fists chest-high before dropping them stiffly to her sides.

"It's okay," Clarence said. "I just don't want you to get sick."

The woman's expression didn't change. "I don't want to have to call the police, sir. But I will."

"No, really," he said, "it's okay. I used to live right there, and this was my tree—"

"Sir."

Then, she stared at him. Feeling uncomfortable, Clarence took a few steps away, looking back and up.

Thinking he saw one of the branches move like a little girl had shifted her weight, he called Lucy's name.

No answer, and the woman was still glaring at him, so he walked to his car. Getting in, he saw that the woman had followed him at a distance, and was circling the car. She had a scrap of paper and a pencil and was writing something. The two children had stayed near the trees, one of them looking up, like maybe he'd seen or heard something. Clarence thought about going over and asking the little boy if Lucy had said anything, but the woman was still standing behind the car, and had pulled out her cell phone. She'd turned out to not be as friendly as Clarence had first thought. She probably wouldn't like him talking to her kids.

Starting the car, Clarence drove away.

22

Traffic had turned stop and go on Six Mile, and Clarence inched along, thinking about Lucy.

If she wasn't at the park, maybe she'd gone back to the apartment. Her mother had never let her go to school, and it didn't seem like the family had ever gone anywhere, done anything. Surely, Victoria had taken Lucy out on errands, to the grocery store, maybe the cleaners, or even the pharmacy – but maybe not. After all, Lucy hadn't run away to any of those places. She'd gone to a half-remembered dream park.

So she must be back at the apartment. Clarence pressed the brake, wishing everyone would hurry up or get out of his way. He needed to know that Lucy was okay.

Then again, she could still be out in the fog, lost. It was actually pretty doubtful that she'd go back to the apartment. It had been a mess. Something bad had happened.

Clarence hadn't been there to help her.

It wasn't his fault alone. Her father hadn't been there either.

Clarence's jaw clenched and he revved the car's engine, needing to stomp on the brake to keep from hitting the person in front of him. He'd wanted to make this left turn, but the person ahead of him had stopped on the yellow light.

It was Richard's fault in the first place. Victoria had found him, offered him the chance to be with his family again, and he hadn't taken it.

Clarence felt the same sinking feeling, the same elated machine-gun heartbeat as when he'd decided to stand up to Mr. Caruthers after he'd been fired.

Thinking about Mr. Caruthers deflated him, and Clarence's shoulders slumped.

Still, Richard needed to know what was going on and be reminded of his responsibilities. Clarence would call Bob O'Neil and get Richard's number—no, his address would be better. Once he knew the full situation, Clarence was sure that Richard would help his daughter, and then Clarence could sleep at night.

But first, he needed to know that Lucy was okay.

He pulled his car into a spot in front of his building and got out. After wiping down the car handle, he started up the sidewalk, then stopped when he saw the mailman walking away from his door. He was bundled up against the chill, but his gloves were fingerless, probably to make it easier to handle the mail. But he didn't know that Clarence hadn't cleaned the doorknob when he'd left his apartment earlier.

"Excuse me," Clarence said, and the man stopped, looked around. Clarence hesitated, then asked, "Do you have any hand sanitizer?"

The mailman grinned. "You bet your ass I do! Never can be too careful carrying around the germs of half the freaking world every day." He dug in his pocket, pulled out a bottle and held it out.

"Oh, I have some. I meant—" Clarence paused. "I forgot to clean my door when I left earlier."

The mailman blinked, his eyes wide, then he burst out laughing. "Guess I better sanitize then. Never can be too careful, right?"

Clarence smiled, relieved when the man took off his gloves to squirt sanitizer into his hands, and rubbed them together vigorously.

"Shit! Makes 'em cold, though. Mighty cold."

"Better put your gloves back on then," Clarence said, still smiling. "Just because you have it in your hands doesn't mean you want to catch it."

Again, the mailman looked shocked, but then laughed even harder than before. "Have a nice day, sir." Walking away, he shook his head, chuckling.

Clarence went inside his apartment.

"It's your fault!"

Clarence fell to his knees, his hands over his ears. That didn't help, though. His head pounded with every word.

"I thought you were my friend!"

"Lucy—I am your friend. I just wanted to make sure you were okay."

"You put ideas in my head, that there was something else outside!"

"Please…" he begged, sinking the rest of the way to the floor.

"There was nothing, and then you, and then you left! Again! You always leave!"

Clarence got up, blundered toward the bathroom. His eyes watered, his vision blurred. To his left, he thought he saw someone standing near the sliding patio door. The wall of the hallway blocked them, and he kept going.

Slamming the bathroom door behind him, he leaned against it, panting.

The soft crying came from all around him.

"Help me. Please. You promised."

Opening the door and stumbling back into the hallway, he said, "I'm trying. I'm trying."

"We need you!"

Clarence felt knocked back by the force of her voice. Losing his balance, he caught himself on the wall, but couldn't help but slide to the floor. He crawled away from the bedrooms and collapsed onto his stomach in the living room beside the chair.

"Come home."

Someone knocked on the door.

Raising and cocking his head, Clarence was puzzled. It had sounded weird. Maybe one of his neighbors had heard the commotion and come to check on him. No, they'd probably called the cops instead. It might be Detective Brennen. Clarence got up to his hands and knees.

It was Bob O'Neil, standing on the other side of the glass patio door. Seeing his tenant, Bob waved.

Out of habitual courtesy, Clarence waved back, though he sagged and almost fell again. Bob looked concerned as Clarence rose to his feet, crossed the room and slid the door open.

"Clarence, are you okay?" Bob asked. He shivered theatrically, asked, "Can I come in?"

Clarence didn't move to open the screen door. Sounding tired, he said, "No. I'm sorry. The place is a mess right now."

Bob looked at what he could see of the apartment. "Look, Clarence, I can understand why you're upset, but really, it's quite cold out here."

Sighing, he said, "I can't risk it. I'm sorry."

"Okay," Bob said. "You're more than upset. I can understand that. I suppose it was wrong to not fully disclose what happened, but I assumed that you had researched the building and were okay… with…"

Trailing off, he looked away.

"You're lying," Clarence said, stomach fluttering at his bold statement.

Bob nodded. "I'm sorry. I never was a good liar. Horrible at poker. I had hoped that you'd never find out. Five months, people would come, they'd seem interested, but then they'd find out and I'd keep calling but they wouldn't call back—"

Realizing he was rambling, Bob cut himself off, then said, "I'm sorry. I just wanted to tell you that, and say if there's anything I can do—"

"Give me Richard Monroe's address."

Bob's mouth hung open. "But I—no! I can't"

"Yes," Clarence said, adrenaline pumping into his system. He would make Bob tell him, even if he had to touch him, make him sick, and he felt a thrill shiver his spine.

He would do it for Lucy.

"Clarence," Bob almost whined. "It's illegal. I can't give out a resident's forwarding address. If he's unlisted, then he wouldn't want that information given out."

Clarence was about to open the screen, leap on Bob, force his infectious fingers into his mouth, when he had an idea.

"Does everyone know what happened?"

Bob stuttered, didn't say anything.

"I'd move out, even if it was next door or downstairs. Was everyone told what happened, or did you not disclose that?"

Bob's voice was small. "I could lose my job."

Clarence folded his arms across his chest.

Bob's shoulders sagged. "I have to go back to the office. I'll call you in ten minutes."

"Five," Clarence said, feeling that shiver again.

Bob hesitated, then nodded. He stepped off the patio, around the bushes, and walked across the parking lot.

Clarence uncrossed his arms, took a deep breath, smiled. A soft moan tickling his ear, he grimaced. The clothes on his right side pressed against his body as the empty air snuggled close to him.

"You're such a strong man."

Clarence jolted away. "Lucy?"

She pushed up to him again. "Shh. She's not here right now."

Clarence relaxed, but only slightly. "Where is she?"

No answer, just a warm feeling like a hand on his cheek.

"I'm doing this for her," Clarence said. "She

needs a father."

The phone rang at the same time that Clarence stumbled, thinking she'd pushed him. That was fine, though. He answered the phone.

"Bob?"

"Yes. Please, I'm pretty sure this is illegal."

"Bob."

He sighed. "Do you have a pen?"

23

After mapping the address, Clarence drove to Huntington Woods. The apartment building he stopped in front of looked nicer than his. Double-checking the address, Clarence got out of his car, walked up to the door and knocked.

Clarence looked around, heard a sound from the other side of the door, a bang like someone had stumbled into it.

"I said no reporters. You got questions, my lawyer—talk to my lawyer."

"Mr. Monroe?" There was no answer. "Mr. Monroe, I'm not a reporter. I just want to talk to you about your wife and daughter."

"Sound like a reporter." His words were liquid, blended into each other.

Clarence didn't know what to say to that. After a while, he said, "I'm not."

There was no answer for a few, long moments. Finally, Richard said, "So? What d'you want?"

"I just have some things that you need to know."

After another long pause, the door clicked. Richard's face was slack and jowly, a scar on his cheek. In his hand, he held a glass, half-empty, ice clinking inside. His eyes were red and unfocused, but he made a show of looking Clarence from head to toe, then back up.

"Yeah. C'mon in."

Richard left the door ajar and wandered back into the apartment. Pushing through the door and closing it behind him, Clarence wiped the knob clean. Keeping his palms pressed against his thighs, he followed Richard.

Even though it was still light out, the apartment's windows faced east and it was dark. Richard hadn't turned on any lights, so Clarence tripped over something that he couldn't see. After a few more feet, he tripped again.

"Can you turn a light on? I can't see," Clarence said.

"Yeah. Sorry."

A lamp clicked on next to Richard who sat in a chair, cradling his drink in his lap. Clarence was standing next to a loveseat, so he sat, keeping his shoulders held as close to him as best he could.

The two men stared at each other.

"So," Richard said. "You said you had some things I need to know."

"Yes—"

"You from the corner?" Richard grunted. "Coroner."

"No, I'm not."

"New evidence?" Richard interrupted again. "You think I'm guilty. I'm guilty. I'm innocent. Now I'm guilty again? You people don't fucking understand." He took a drink, then said, "I loved her. Them. Both of them."

"I understand, Mr. Monroe." Clarence nodded.

"They don't," Richard said. "You wanna know, but you don't wanna understand."

"I want to understand," Clarence said, and he did. He felt something like déjà vu talking to Richard.

The scar on Richard's face disappeared into a dimple when he smiled, his lips pursed, tears brimming his eyes. None of them had wanted to understand, except this man. Richard's breath came short. His voice was low, almost ashamed.

"We got together junior year. Friend's girlfriend had a friend, so they said I should come to a dance. I didn't have anything else to do, you know, so yeah, I went.

"Matt and his girlfriend left me hanging, but she said it was okay, she'd shown Victoria my picture, even though my hair looked stupid. So she found me, and she looked pretty hot. I was scared of that, but she seemed cool.

"So, I'm not really sure what happened. We started talking and Matt's girlfriend was smiling, he was giving me the thumb's up and I was thinking, yeah, this is pretty cool. I don't think she heard a word I said. It was so loud."

Richard grew quiet, his face puzzled. "Had a dream about it couple nights ago. Except she looked how she had—" He shuddered. "Woke up like I was gonna have a heart attack."

Clarence sat forward in the chair. "This dream—"

Richard kept talking over Clarence. "We

started dating—I'm not even sure how. It'd be like, I go somewhere to hang out with Matt, and his girlfriend would be there with Victoria. Soon, everyone was calling her my girlfriend, and she didn't seem to mind, so…"

"Went to college, no big whoop. Business degree and my dad said I could come work for him, so that worked out, I guess."

Richard stopped talking to finish his drink, refilling it from a mostly-empty bottle that sat on the table next to his chair.

"Mr. Monroe—"

"We got married the year we graduated. We'd been—you know, sleeping together a couple years, and I told her I loved her and she said it back, so we got married. We were living in my parents' upstairs loft and everything seemed okay."

Richard's voice cracked, startling Clarence. Richard hadn't been speaking to him, had just been talking, his eyes unfocused. Now he looked at Clarence, his eyes intense.

"There were signs, you know." One hand clenched around the glass, the other on the arm of the chair. "But I didn't want to believe something was wrong with my wife. Who does, right? Even before Lucy was born, everything became about *should.* I should get a job other than at Dad's. She should be a stay-at-home mother. We should get a place of our own. Lucy should be home-schooled. She seemed to know what we should be doing, so I kind of just let her take the lead.

"Like this one time, about a month before—" He cleared his throat and took a drink. "She starts bugging me about the people upstairs. They're too loud, she says. Always making so much noise she thought the ceiling was going to collapse. She wanted me to call Bob, our landlord."

Clarence twitched at the name.

"I tell her the office is closed by the time I get home, why doesn't she do it. And she gets all mad and says the man should take care of things like that.

"Couple nights later, I come home and she's standing on the table, hands against the ceiling, and she starts screaming when I walk in the door, "The ceiling! The ceiling!" So I make a big show of calling Bob and leaving a message, even though there's an emergency number. I thought she was just being melodramatic to, you know, get my attention."

Richard drank and drew a deep, shuddering breath. "I didn't want to see, you know. The way her knuckles were white, her arms trembling like she'd been there for a while. Lucy was in her bedroom. Alright, but she wouldn't talk about what had happened. Victoria never asked if Bob called back."

He leaned forward. His eyes seemed to be pleading with Clarence. "I didn't want to see."

Clarence thought of his mother and had no sympathy to offer.

There were scars on Richard's trembling hands, two on the left and one on the right. The one on his right slashed across the back, from his wrist to between the knuckles of his first and middle fingers. The ones on his left were smaller, crisscrossing and Clarence could imagine Richard's hands over his face, blood running from the gouge in his cheek, trying to protect it from the quick, jabbing flicks of the knife in Victoria's hand.

Richard saw him looking and touched his cheek. "I came home and she was just sitting on the couch. I walked right past her. I needed to piss like a race horse." His voice started cracking, and he breathed in gasps. "The curtain—was pulled and I thought, "It's never—pulled…" Lucy's eyes were still open."

Clarence couldn't look at him. The apartment around him had nothing on the walls, no books on the shelves, only boxes. A man didn't live here; he existed.

"She sat there like—like nothing was wrong and I tried—to talk—talk to her but it was like—I wasn't there so I yelled—I started yelling and she wasn't looking at me—so I grabbed her—her arm shot out…"

Clarence knew. The first of twenty-seven stab wounds, this one the worst. Had the blade not lodged in Richard's shoulder joint and snapped off, leaving only half an inch still on the handle, he'd probably be dead as well.

Richard wiped his face. "I've told that story so many times—everyone wanted to know. Parents, cops, the trial, reporters, and I kept telling it, and every time, it seemed like it wasn't real more and more." He slammed the rest of his drink and came down with unfocused eyes. "Sometimes I feel like I'm not really here. Like she's still looking through me."

After Richard was silent for a while, Clarence cleared his throat. Richard blinked, looked at him.

"Mr. Monroe, I'm sorry. But there's something you should know…"

Richard nodded.

Clarence didn't know how to put it, so he blurted, "You can still be a good dad. Your daughter needs you."

"What?" Richard asked, sitting up.

Clarence smoothed his pants. His hands had started to sweat.

"Lucy needs you. She needs your help. She's in danger. Victoria is—"

"What? What are you talking about?"

"Victoria is hurting your daughter. I think you can help her. Lucy told me that Victoria found you and—"

"Who told you that?" Richard's flushed face went white. "No. That was just a dream. I saw her picture in court, her arm, and I…"

"I thought so too, but—"

"Get out."

Richard rose unsteadily, ice clinking in his empty glass. Clarence stood too, stepping away from Richard when he lurched forward.

"I don't think there's much time. Victoria was pushing against me and I think—"

With a surprised mixture of grunt and growl, Richard threw his glass at Clarence, missing widely. Clarence ducked and took a few more steps away from

Richard, who grabbed the bottle from the table and swung it at Clarence. Misjudging the distance, Richard overbalanced and fell.

Clarence crept a little closer, wanting to help, but unwilling to touch him. Richard had already suffered enough. He was crying when he pushed himself up onto his knees.

"Get out!"

Richard held the last word, though it sounded like an empty echo, chasing Clarence out of the house with it.

Hurrying back to his car, Clarence drove back home.

24

It was up to him now. Lucy didn't have anyone else.

He could walk away, find another apartment and move. He didn't think either Lucy or her mother would be able to find him if they didn't know where to look. It would be that easy. He'd just lost his job. He'd probably need to move anyway.

Except that he wouldn't.

Pulling into Applewood's parking lot, he didn't see the beige, non-descript sedan.

Clarence needed to figure out a way to help Lucy permanently. The only way to do that was to get her away from her mother.

She had found the park by herself, at least the tree that she and Clarence had sat in. So, reasonably, Clarence could take her somewhere, show her the place, tell her as many details as he could think of to make it real for her, and then she'd be able to stay there. He'd visit her every night so they could play together. Maybe even tell her more about Mickey so she wouldn't get lonely when he wasn't around.

Clarence opened his apartment door, cleaned the outside knob, and went inside. Deep in thought, he didn't see Detective Brennen getting out of the sedan.

Victoria wouldn't be happy, and she'd take it out on him. He thought he'd be able to handle it. All she'd ever done was scare him that one time he thought she was his mother or try to seduce him. Once Lucy was comfortably wherever she was going to be, he would be free to move to another apartment.

Victoria would still be there though, and the next person to move in would be left to deal with her.

Clarence's stomach knotted. He didn't like leaving a mess. No, he needed a solution for Victoria as well.

Clarence stood just inside the door, waiting. His apartment was silent. Deciding that he couldn't wait to fall asleep, he started toward the bathroom to tell Lucy about his plan so far. Maybe she would have an idea of what would make her mother happy.

On his way past the living room, he checked the answering machine. The light was blinking, so he pressed the button.

"Clarence, this Bob O'Neil. A Detective Brennen just stopped by my office—"

A heavy knocking came from the front door. Clarence froze.

"—looking for you. I told him that I had no idea when you'd be back, that you were even out. He left his number…"

The recorded Bob paused while the knocking continued.

"Clarence if this is about—what we were talking about earlier—I don't think there's any need to—I don't even know what calling the cops would do. But anyway, why don't you give me a call before you call him."

"Clarence Gottlieb!"

Clarence recognized Brennen's voice.

"Clarence, open the door immediately. You are wanted for questioning for your involvement with the death of James Caruthers. I have a warrant for your arrest."

Clarence's mind was blank, his thoughts a high-pitched buzz. His vision blurring, he felt himself falling, but stumbled and caught himself.

"They'll never leave us alone," she whispered into his ear.

That startled Clarence back into conscious thought. He was under arrest. The police thought that he had murdered Mr. Caruthers, and they were right. He was a horrible liar, Brennen already knew after talking with him for five minutes. They'd find out about Val, what had happened the day before he'd killed Mr. Caruthers. They'd say he was going crazy, becoming more violent with each passing day. They'd find out about him causing his mother's death, and that would be the nail in his coffin. It was a pattern of behavior, they'd say, starting when he was young. He'd go to jail where he would probably kill one cellmate after another until they'd have no choice but to keep him in solitary confinement until the day he died.

Finally, the world would be kept safe from Clarence's germs.

"Help me, please," she said.

He deserved to be punished. Of course he felt bad about the men who would get sick and die from being his cellmate, but they were criminals and their lives were a small price to pay for being at peace for the first time since his mother had died.

After a pause to allow Clarence to answer, Brennen recommenced pounding on the door.

It was tempting to give himself up, but only briefly.

He needed to help Lucy. There was no one else.

First, he needed to stall Brennen. He went over to the door.

"Detective," he said, then needed to repeat himself when the knocking didn't stop. "I understand. I need to get some things, and I'll be right out."

Clarence spoke loudly, as if he believed that Brennen wouldn't be able to hear him otherwise, sliding the chain into place.

"Mr. Gottlieb, you don't need to bring anything."

Clarence dragged the chair over to the door as quietly as he could. "Not even a toothbrush?"

"What?"

"Well, I better grab a toothbrush and a change of clothes, just in case," Clarence said while he wedged the chair between the door and the half-wall of the entryway.

That should take care of Brennen. Clarence worried briefly about him breaking through a window when he realized Clarence wasn't coming out, but there was nothing he could do about that.

Clarence started to sweat. He didn't know what was going to happen. Even when he'd come up with his plan to relocate Lucy, he hadn't been certain of it. But at least he thought he'd have time to find a way to make it work. He'd hoped that Lucy would be patient with him while he built a world around her, for her.

It might have worked, given time.

Clarence didn't have any more time, but there was one way he could protect Lucy that he was almost positive would work.

He hadn't cleaned the apartment in a day and half. When Brennen finally managed to break his way in, he'd be exposed to high levels of Clarence's germs. Clarence felt a cramp of guilt for that, but there was nothing he could do about it now. He just hoped that the other policemen who came would wear gloves.

Clarence hurried to the bathroom, shut the door behind him, locked it. He also locked the other door that led into the walk-in closet in his bedroom.

Everything was still in the bathroom from when he'd cleaned the shower yesterday. A soft smell of bleach and ammonia lingered in the air, and he inhaled deeply, a small smile on his face.

Turning on the hot water, steam rose, hanging in the air. He dropped the stopper into the drain, allowing his mind to be calmed by the sound of rushing water.

Clarence emptied the bottle of bleach into the water first. Then, he upended the bottle of ammonia. Almost immediately, he became dizzy, his head swimming.

He couldn't hear the sound of the door breaking over the sound of water.

Clarence wondered what it would feel like, what it would be like once it was over.

His knees felt like water as he leaned against the wall and slid down. The air was clearer, and he took a deep breath, coughed it out.

The steam filled the room.

25

“Welcome home,” she said.

About the Author

Sean M Davis was born and raised in Detroit. He went to Wayne State University, majoring in English, and has attended several workshops, including the Borderlands Press Writers Boot Camp. His stories, poetry, and nonfiction have been published in Borderlands 6, Silent Screams, Amanda's Recurring Nightmare, on Fangoria.com as a finalist in their first Weird Words contest, and elsewhere.

Made in the USA
Columbia, SC
27 November 2023